The Kabbalah Killings

The Kabbalah Killings

A MURDER MYSTERY INTRODUCTION TO JEWISH
MYSTICISM

A Solomon Hunter Educational Murder Mystery
Illustrated by the Author

Arthur Asa Berger

PulpLit Publishing
Needham, Massachusetts

PulpLit Publishing
762 South St.
Needham, MA
www.PulpLit.com

Cover Design by Diego Linares

The Image of the 10 Sefirot used with the kind permission of
Eliezer Segal, University of Calgary

Illustrated by the author.

This book was lovingly typeset using LaTeX

First American Edition 2004

Library of Congress Control Number: 2004096419
ISBN: 0-9746196-2-0

10 9 8 7 6 5 4 3 2 1

Preface

The Kabbalah Killings is a novel that deals with two mysteries. The first mystery involves finding who killed Professor Azriel Moshe, the leader of an interdisciplinary team investigating the effects (medical, psychological, and so on) of the Kabbalah on those who study it. The second mystery involves the Kabbalah itself; what is the Kabbalah, what are its basic beliefs, and why does it grip people's imaginations and have such a hold on its adherents? Why have people been fascinated by it for thousands of years?

While writing this book, I made considerable use of a number of works such as Daniel G. Matt's *The Essential Kabbalah: The Heart of Jewish Mysticism* (Harper Collins, 1996)and his translation of *The Zohar: The Book of Enlightenment* (Paulist Press, 1983). I also made use of Gershom Scholem's *Major Trends in Jewish Mysticism* (originally published in 1946 by Schocken Books), *The Universal Jewish Encyclopedia* (published in 1940), and various Web sites on the Kabbalah—of which there are thousands. I would also like to thank Eliezer Segal of the University of Calgary for his kind permission to use his representation of *The Image of the 10 Sefirot.*

I became interested in the Kabbalah after taking a course on the subject with Rabbi Lavey Derby of Congregation Kol Shofar in Tiburon. I owe him a debt of gratitude for introducing me to the subject and for teaching a very lively and exciting course.

Contents

Personae

Azriel Moshe, Professor of Psychiatry
A Bostonian, transplanted to California, who is Professor of psychiatry at the University of California at San Francisco medical school. He attended Harvard for both his undergraduate degree and medical training. He is investigating whether the Kabbalah is efficacious in helping people with physical and mental illnesses. Some of his associates think he has a serious case of both kinds of illnesses himself and that overly zealous Kabbalistic study may be a contributing factor. He has put together an interdisciplinary team of scholars to pursue his investigation.

Leon Gerhard, Anglo-American Rabbi
An English rabbi who is an expert on the Kabbalah and part of the interdisciplinary Kabbalah team assembled by Azriel Moshe. He has a doctorate is in psychology from Cambridge University and teaches psychology at the University of California at Berkeley.

Svetlana Pagetsky, Russian Historian
A beautiful, 35-year-old red-headed Russian historian educated at Tartu University, whose interest in the Kabbalah extends from its theoretical aspects to its practitioners. She has been divorced twice and is a woman with legions of lovers and admirers, one of whom was the victim.

Jean-Pascal Dovet, French Neurologist

A divorced, middle-aged, French neurologist who is a visiting professor at the medical school investigating Jewish mysticism and various other matters of neurological interest. His medical training was at the University of Paris and Johns Hopkins University.

Krista Scelba, Sociologist of Religion

A vivacious and attractive Italian sociologist of religion who is investigating mysticism, the Kabbalah in particular, and its relation to physical and mental health. She did her undergraduate work at the "Red" University—the University of Milan—and got her Ph.D. at the University of Rome. She may have had a relationship with Azriel Moshe and may be having one with another member of the team.

Solomon Hunter, Inspector, San Francisco Police

Hunter specializes in cases involving murdered murderous professors. His academic cases have involved professors of postmodernism, mass media theory, cultural studies, and literary analysis. He has a particular talent for making suspects involved in murder cases underestimate him.

Talcott Weems, Sergeant, San Francisco Police

Hunter's assistant and an anti-intellectual with a particular loathing for literary scholars, postmodernists, mass communication theorists, and professors in all disciplines. He isn't sophisticated, but he's got a good head on his shoulders.

The Zohar is written in pseudepigraphic form, almost one might say, in the form of a mystical novel. In itself, this is not a new departure in style; the pseudepigraphic form has been employed by many previous writers, including Kabbalists. Authors of the book *Bahir* made use of the literary device and spoke through the mouths of older authorities—some of them mere names of fiction, such as Rabbi Amora or Rabbi Rehumai. But neither before nor since has any Kabbalist shown anything like the same delight in letting his fancy elaborate upon the details of his mystification. Against the background of an imaginative Palestinian setting, Rabbi Simeon ben Yohai is seen wandering about with his son Eleazar, his friend, and his disciples, and discoursing on all manner of things human and divine. (1946:157)

- Gershom Sholem, *Major Trends in Jewish Mysticism*

1

The Death of Azriel Moshe

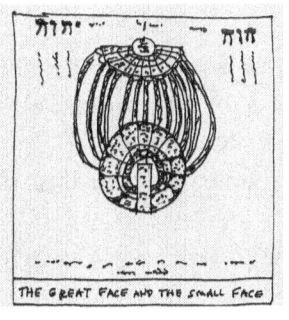

THE GREAT FACE AND THE SMALL FACE

The rose. The key to the Kabbalah is the rose. I know that now. The rose will enable me to penetrate the secrets of the Zohar and the Kabbalah. Like a giant onion, with layer upon layer guarding an inner kernel, the secrets remain a mystery. There are thirteen paths between the Great Face and the Small Face. Will I ever understand their hidden meaning?

"What do you think it means?" asked Hunter, reading from Professor Azriel Moshe's black, leather-bound journal.

Sergeant Weems looked at him with a blank stare.

"It obviously has something to do with this Kabbalah stuff the Professor was involved in," Weems replied. "The Kabbalah's mystical, isn't it? And fashionable, too. I read in the paper that Madonna is studying the Kabbalah. The passage you read sounds like the Professor had discovered that roses play some role in the Kabbalah. I can't figure out what a rose has to do with the Kabbalah...or is it the Zohar? Or what the stuff about great faces and small faces is about. But Professor Moshe seemed to think a rose would help him unlock the mystery. I don't know. Professors seem to be getting crazier and crazier. They get paid too much, that's the trouble. They hardly do any work nowadays and have too much time to get into mischief."

"Professor Moshe scribbled something on the floor with his own blood," said Hunter, pointing . "It looks like it might be the beginning of some kind of a Hebrew letter."

"God only knows," said Weems.

"Have you been able to find out anything about the suspects?" asked Hunter.

"We've got the intelligence unit looking for info," said Weems. "Do you think Professor Moshe might have been into some sort of sex triangle?"

"Who can say?" replied Hunter. "I assume the technicians took photos of the body and have dusted for fingerprints...all that routine stuff. And the autopsy is going to be done soon?"

"Yes," said Weems. "We'll have photos for you in a short while."

Solomon Hunter picked up a phone in Professor Moshe's office, and punched in a number.

"I'm calling the Professor's secretary," he told Weems. "She was really hysterical shortly after the murder." Weems nodded in understanding. After a few seconds, Hunter was connected.

"Hello," he said. "This is Inspector Solomon Hunter from the San Francisco Police Department. Will you please arrange for the members of Professor Moshe's work group—or whatever it was—to get together in the seminar room next to the one in which he was murdered. I'd like to have a few minutes with them. I'd also like to use his study to speak with each one of them privately. I'm afraid that nobody on the Kabbalah study team will be able to go anywhere for a while."

Hunter hung up the phone.

"She's going to take care of everything. Weems, let's go over the facts again so I can get this case in my head. I'm still not clear about everything that happened."

Weems flipped through his notes, and began reading. "At twelve thirty-three this morning, the rabbi's secretary, a woman named Felliyanka November, called 911," said Weems. "Do you want me to read the transcript?"

Hunter shook his head. "Just summarize."

"She was hysterical. She went into his office, where Professor Moshe had been meeting with his colleagues, and discovered he'd been stabbed in the back with a silver stiletto. He'd collapsed onto the floor, seemingly dead. Her office is between the Professor's office and the seminar room where they were meeting during the morning. There was another door leading to the corridor.

"It appers that in the last few seconds of his life," Weems continued, "Moshe made a strange mark on the floor with his own blood. Mrs. November came in, she said, because she thought she heard strange noises coming from the Professor's office. He was supposed to be having lunch somewhere. Just before she opened the door to his office, she thought she heard the door to the corridor close. When she walked into the room and found him dead on the floor, she started screaming. Other professors came running. She picked up the phone, dialed 911, and reported a homicide at room 665 of the William Fry science building at the UC Medical Campus."

"I arrived here at the campus in about ten or fifteen minutes," Weems continued. "I brought some officers and a few technicians from the forensics team with me and they started doing their stuff. The victim was lying on his stomach. There was a knife stuck in his back and a pool of blood on the floor. The index finger on his left hand was red from the blood he used to scrawl the mark, as you can see. It seems, from what some of the people who were here told me, that he'd just had a meeting with the team of researchers whom he'd been working with earlier in the morning. They were trying to find out whether studying the Kabbalah might have any medical benefits. The victim's team of experts met all morning and then, around noon, they broke for lunch. Sometime during the lunch period, someone killed him."

"I guess the Kabbalah didn't have any medical benefits for him, did it?" said Hunter.

Weems gave a tight smile, and flipped his notebook shut.

The hidden God, *En-Sof,* manifests himself to the Kabbalist under ten different aspects, which in turn comprise an endless variety of shades and gradations. Every grade has its own symbolic name, in strict accordance with its peculiar manifestations. Their sum total constitutes a highly complex symbolical structure, in which almost every Biblical word corresponds to one of the Sefiroth.... The mystical conception of the Torah, of which mention has been made... is fundamental for the understanding of the peculiar symbolism of the Zohar. The Torah is conceived of as a vast *corpus symbolicum* representative of the hidden life in God which the theory of the Sefiroth attempts to describe. For the mystic who starts out with this assumption, every word is capable of becoming a symbol, and the most inconspicuous phrases or verses are precisely the ones into which at times the greatest importance is read. (1946:209-210)

- Gershom Sholem, *Major Trends in Jewish Mysticism*

2

The Kabbalah Research Team

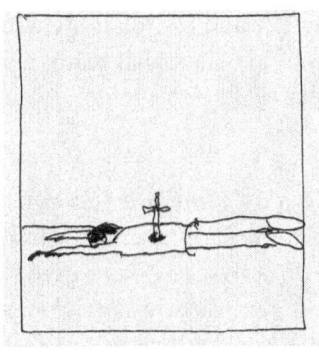

"Find out who met with him this morning," said Hunter. "Who's on his team or his research group? Whatever they call it. While you're at it, get a record of all his phone calls—both incoming and outgoing—over the last few months. See if his secretary kept a calendar of his appointments, that kind of thing."

"I've already got a list of the members of his research team," said Weems. "His secretary, Mrs. November, gave the list to me, along with a group photograph they had taken when they were just getting started. They're from all over the world. In addition to Professor Moshe, who's from America, there's an English psychologist on the team named Leon Gerhard. There's a Russian scholar, Svetlana Pagetsky, a French neurologist named Jean-Pascal Dovet, and a sociologist of religion from Italy named Krista Scelba."

"It's like the United Nations," said Hunter. "But this place has all kinds of people coming here for various periods of time. I had a case here a number of years ago. Same kind of thing. People from all over the world."

Hunter glanced at his watch.

"In a while it will be time to meet the members of the Kabbalah medical study group. Make sure you have some men guarding them. We'll interview each of them separately to see what light they can shed on this killing. And on the mark Moshe left on the floor. Something about this murder is different, but I can't put my finger on it. Take, for example, his journal. Was the killer after the journal? Maybe he... or she... didn't have time to grab it because they heard Mrs. November coming. Or maybe it had nothing to do with his murder... There may be some information hidden away in it that sheds light on who the killer was."

"If it's his diary, it may show a motive," Weems said.

Hunter picked up the journal and opened it.

"He starts by talking about the weather and his relations with someone. Then he says some stuff about his Kabbalah team, and then something on some esoteric aspect of Jewish theology. Let me read it to you:

The sun is shining and it's a lovely day. Too bad I'm not in a better mood today...I've had very bad news lately, and my relations with my "rose" seem to be getting worse. There doesn't seem to be anything I can do about it. It's very distressing. I must find a way to put this matter out of mind and return to my Kabbalah research. My team doesn't seem to be getting anywhere. There are interminable discussions of the most trivial things. We haven't even framed an acceptable research plan. Leon is such an ass. He's so steeped in his historical approach to things and has so much to say about everything that it's difficult to make any progress. Most of the time, Jean-Pascal just sits there with that stupid expression on his face, gazing at Svetlana, lost in his dreams about her. I think she's involved, somehow, with Krista. The modern world is truly perplexing. It's all too complicated for words.

I'm beginning to wonder whether this interdisciplinary team business is going to work. Instead of getting insights from different perspectives, I seem to be getting the worst of all worlds—people from different disciplines and callings who think their perspective is the only one worth considering. I guess that's the trouble with academics. We each think that our discipline is the most important one and that people in our discipline are the smartest people at the university.

I need the Kabbalah to calm my nerves. I need the rose. What is it that Moses Cordovero wrote, 'In the beginning Ein Sof emanated ten Sefirot, which are of its essence, united with it. It and they are entirely one.' Yes, not like my tea party full of mad hatters. 'Ein Sof is present in all things in actuality, while all things are present in it potentially.' Very good. If only I could call forth the unerasable names, the Sefirot. If only I could lose myself in the Zohar *and in the Sefirot!*

Fortunately, I've got a good sense of humor. When you deal with a group of people, each of whom is full of himself or herself, things never go smoothly. Maybe this whole venture should be looked upon as a comedy.

"What in the hell is that all about?" asked Weems. "Who is this *Ein Sof* character? What are Sefirot? What's all this stuff about unerasable names?"

"Come on, now, Weems," said Hunter. "The Jews are entitled to have their own mystical tradition, just like the Christians and the Muslims. If Christians have wine turning into blood, why can't the Jews have unerasable names and these ten Sefirot—whatever they are. Who knows? The Kabbalah may even hold a clue to this murder. We should examine this journal carefully."

"You're going to read a couple of hundred pages of nonsense from that guy's journal? You'll be as nutty as a fruitcake by the time you finish," replied Weems.

"I'm also going to find out more about the Kabbalah. I have a hunch it might help us crack this case," replied Hunter. "So far, there's only one thing that all the members of this team have in common—and that's the Kabbalah."

"By the time your done, you'll be spouting Hebrew, living on bean curd, and running around in a black coat with a big black hat, collecting money in Union Square like the Lubavichers. Crazier things have happened," said Weems.

"The Orthodox Jews like meat," replied Hunter, smiling. "They say there's a commandment in the Bible for them to eat meat. But if this Kabbalah is a front for a cult and they brainwash me, I give you permission to arrest me, lock me up somewhere, and have someone deprogram me. But I don't think you have to worry about anything like that happening."

"Yeah, you're right. If the postmodernists couldn't drive you batty, nobody can."

Hunter laughed. "They were quite a collection of characters, weren't they? If I remember correctly, they were also part of an interdisciplinary team—except that it was involved with postmodernism, not the Kabbalah."

"Ah yes, the case of the *Postmortem for a Postmodernist*. I wonder, could postmodernists be Kabbalists?" asked Weems.

"Why not? They seem to think everything is connected to postmodernism the same way the Kabbalists think, I'd be willing to bet, that everything is connected to the Kabbalah—whatever it is," said Hunter.

"We also have to remember that everyone in this interdisciplinary team could be in danger," added Hunter. "Remember that crazy lit Professor from Berkeley who killed off the entire editorial board of his Shakespeare journal because he thought they were going to replace him?"

"Academics are the most ruthless murderers," said Weems. "They're too smart for their own good."

"Which makes the murderer in this case exceedingly dangerous," added Hunter. "Smart murderers are more devious and more dangerous than dumb ones."

"I'll get you whatever info our research people can get on the characters involved with this team," said "Weems. "You can erase their names, one by one, when you're sure they're innocent. When you get to an unerasable name, like the one that poor Professor Moshe was looking for, you'll know you've hit paydirt."

The Hebrew word *kabbalah* means "receiving" or "that which has been received." On the one hand, Kabbalah refers to tradition, ancient wisdom received and treasured from the past. On the other hand, if one is truly receptive, wisdom appears spontaneously, unprecedented, taking you by surprise.

The Jewish mystical tradition combines both of these elements. Its vocabulary teems with what the *Zohar*—the canonical text of the Kabbalah—calls "new-ancient words." Many of its formulations derive from traditional sources—the Bible and rabbinic literature—but with a twist. For example, "the world that is coming," a traditional phrase often understood as referring to a far-off messianic era, turn into "the world that is constantly coming," constantly flowing, a timeless dimension of reality available right here and now, if one is receptive. (1996:1)

- Daniel C. Matt, *The Essential Kabbalah: The Heart of Jewish Mysticism*

3

Inspector Hunter Meets the Kabbalah Researchers

SOLOMON HUNTER PREPARES TO MEET THE RESEARCH TEAM

The members of the late Azriel Moshe's research team were discussing something loudly when Inspector Hunter entered the seminar room, with Weems trailing behind him. Everyone in the room stopped talking. Hunter was wearing a dark gray Brooks Brothers worsted suit with pin stripes, a light gray Borsolino hat, a striped J. Press shirt with a Silka tie, and black Allan Edmonds shoes. Weems had on a tan poplin suit, a white shirt, a non-descript tie he got at a K-mart, and tan desert boots.

"Good afternoon," said Hunter. He registered each of them in his memory, taking mental photographs. "I'm Inspector Solomon Hunter of the San Francisco Police Department. I'm here to investigate the murder of your colleague, Professor Azriel Moshe. And this is Sergeant Talcott Weems, my associate."

At this, Krista Scelba, a blonde woman who was wearing a lot of makeup, moaned. "My God. What a terrible thing! What a tragedy!" She was trembling.

Hunter paused. His face showed no emotion.

"You're right. A murder is a terrible thing," he said. "I deeply sympathize with you and all of your colleagues."

"We'll assist you in any way possible," said Leon Gerhard, a tall man with brown hair.

"Thank you," said Hunter. Hunter paused dramatically. "It's possible—perhaps even likely—that someone in this room was Azriel's killer."

Hunter looked at each person sitting around the seminar table carefully. They all had different expressions on their faces, from indignation and incredulity to horror and fear.

"You don't really believe that, do you?" said Jean-Pascal Dovet, a dark, swarthy man, with a short beard and mustache. His eyes were a liquid brown. On his face was a curiously animated expression. "You were just saying that for shock value, weren't you?"

"I'm afraid not," he replied. "I've been investigating murders for many years and there are always people who are shocked when I suggest that one of the persons in a room full of suspects might be a murderer. Of course, it's always possible that in this case the murderer was a stranger, that the killing was random, a matter of chance. But more often than not, the murderer knew the victim quite well. We'll find out more about what happened as the investigation proceeds. By the time this investigation is over, I'll know a great deal about each of you."

Hunter paused and surveyed the people in the room once again. He smiled. "It's always like this," he thought, "when you have a group of people who are involved, one way or another, in a murder case. The expressions of surprise and shock, the mock outrage. But always, in the end, behind their expression of bewilderment, one person is a ruthless killer." They were looking at him with curiosity, trying desperately to take his measure.

"I've not had the benefit of the amount of education you've all had, though I'm a graduate of the University of California at Berkeley, but in my job, we learn a number of interesting and curious things about people that you don't find out about in psychology courses or textbooks—about human motivations, jealousy, love, passion, fear, the desire for self-preservation, and hatred. One of your colleagues has been murdered and whoever murdered him might, if the situation seems warranted, strike again. So, let me remind you, until we find the killer, each of you is in danger."

"My God!" said the blonde woman with a tremulous voice. "It never occurred to me that he might strike again."

"Or she!" added Hunter. "Our killer might be a woman."

"A woman? It seems so unlike what women do," said Jean-Pascal. "If only Maigret were here; he'd solve the case in no time!"

Hunter smiled. "We have a comedian," he thought.

"Why not Sherlock Holmes? Or Sam Spade?" replied Hunter. "I'm afraid you'll have to settle for me and my assistant, Sergeant Weems. Over the years, we've found ways to get the job done."

Weems nodded.

"He's a specialist in academic murders," Weems volunteered. "He's dealt with postmodernists, cultural theorists, media theorists, literary critics... you name it. Whenever professors start killing one another, the suits in the police department always send Inspector Hunter to find out what's going on. And he's been very successful at it."

"Now, let me explain what will happen," Hunter interrupted. "I will ask you all to remain together in a room that we are obtaining for that purpose. We will have a policeman at the door to protect you. You can call whomever you wish and inform anyone you want that you will be indisposed for a while. I will then speak with each of you to see what I can find out about what happened before the murder and what kind of relations you have with one another. When I'm done questioning all of you, we will release you, but you'll all be under police protection. We'll get together tomorrow morning at 10:00 in this seminar room and I'll give you a progress report on how things are coming along. We will probably want to have another round of questioning tomorrow. Does anyone have any questions?"

"What are you doing with Azriel's body?" asked Svetlana Pagetsky, a beautiful, red-headed woman. "Will there be an autopsy?"

"Yes," replied Hunter. "An autopsy will be conducted either this evening or early tomorrow morning. Those police pathologists can learn an awful lot when they get to work. You'd be amazed."

There was an icy silence in the room.

"We've taken lots of photographs and have dusted the room where Professor Moshe was killed," Hunter continued. "We also have our intelligence unit getting as much information about him, and, I should inform you—about each of you—as they can: from your universities, the police in the cities where you live, your neighbors, and Interpol."

"It may sound terrible to say this," said, Leon Gerhard, the tall man sitting next to the red-headed woman, "but the process you've described is quite fascinating. Perhaps the police investigation should be the dominant metaphor for academic research. We're all investigators trying to find out the truth about various people and situations. Your methods are our methods... you'd have made a very fine addition to our interdisciplinary team, I believe. You have, I would suggest, the soul of an academic."

"Two fools," thought Devot. "I can't imagine they'll get very far with this investigation, unless they're lucky. But in these kinds of things luck may be more important than brains."

"They scare me," thought the swarthy man with the dark beard and mustache. "This inspector seems so pedestrian and such a minor-level bureaucrat, with his canned chitchat. People like that can be very dangerous."

"Hunter's a very strange type," thought Svetlana Pagetsky. "He went to Berkeley and dresses like a college professor. These detectives have, as he pointed out, an arcane street knowledge. They may not be educated or sophisticated, but they can be very shrewd."

Krista Scelba looked at Hunter and smiled. "The police. They are so enigmatic. I can't read him. Is that because there's nothing to read, that he's a cipher, that there's nothing beneath the surface? Or because he keeps himself hidden so beautifully? This should be a very interesting challenge. Very interesting," she thought.

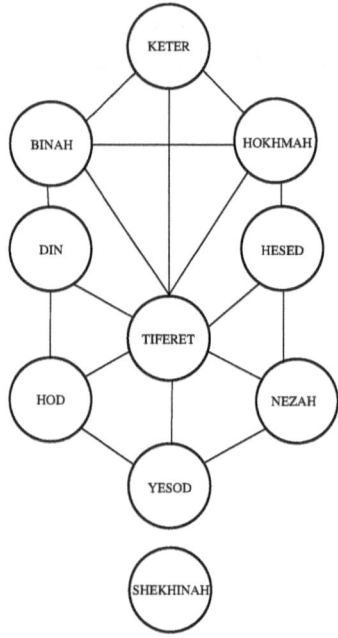

The Sefirot and Associated Names of God

4

The Brain Doctor

"Let's interview Jean-Pascal Dovet first," said Hunter, once all the arrangements had been made and the professors were secure in a faculty lounge. "His comment about Inspector Maigret caught my attention."

"Who's Maigret? A famous French detective?" asked Weems.

"Very famous, but also very imaginary. He's a creation of a French... no, I think it's a Belgian writer, named Simenon. Simenon was incredibly prolific. Some say he was a hack. They say he could write a mystery in two weeks. He must have written two hundred of them. Maybe more. He also claims that he slept with ten thousand different women, including, its rumored, his own daughter."

"So this Dovet is a wise-guy," said Weems. "Making jokes at our expense."

"Some people can't resist. It may be their way of dealing with anxiety and stress. I read an article in *The Chronicle* by some shrink who made that point. Humor in cases like that is a defense mechanism. It helps ward off depression and helps with all kinds of other problems."

Weems stuck his head out into the hall, and asked an officer to bring in Professor Dovet.

Several minutes later there was a light knock on the door. Jean-Pascal Dovet entered and sat down in a chair that had been prepared for him.

"I am first," he said. "But I trust, in this case, first will not be last," he added, smiling.

"This murder doesn't seem to have dampened your mood," said Hunter. "You seem in excellent spirits and are even joking around a bit. I found it interesting that you would make a joke about Maigret just a short while after your colleague, Azriel Moshe, was murdered."

Dovet stroked his beard, and paused before speaking.

"Yes," he replied. "That's true. But that's because I am somewhat of a fatalist, you see. I am a physician and have seen countless people die in my work in the hospitals. Some of them have been my patients, of whom I was quite fond. After a while you learn to accept death—to face it, to put it behind you, and to get on with your life. I'm not the kind of person who gets melancholy about death. God makes the decisions and we carry on as best we can, hoping that he has written us into the book of life and not the book of death. Can you understand that?"

"Yes," said Hunter. "I probably feel somewhat the same way you do about death. It's part of my job. Now, what can you tell me about this team of scholars that Professor Moshe assembled? What were you doing on the team?"

"Azriel Moshe was a brilliant psychiatrist," replied Dovet. "He was educated in Boston, where he was born, and came to the University of California Medical School a number of years ago to teach and conduct research. He comes from a very Orthodox Jewish family—I imagine that's why he was named Azriel. He was interested in Jewish mysticism and was trying to find out whether there was any connection between people who studied the Kabbalah and health, both mental and physical. His theory was that mystics, of all kinds, might have gained some psychological and perhaps even physical benefits from having a belief structure that sustained them. He chose the Kabbalah because of his fascination with it. You know that it has been in vogue, lately. Some Hollywood stars have become involved with it, you know. Like Madonna and even Britney Spears."

"Yes," replied Hunter. "I've read about them in the papers. What exactly is Kabbalah? I don't know much about it except that I understand it's a kind of Jewish mysticism."

"It's hard to know where to begin," replied Dovet. "And hard to explain, because there are so many different things to know and there are so many mystical allusions. The term Kabbalah means, in general terms, 'the reception' or 'that which has been received.' It developed in medieval times. What has been received is a kind of ancient and holy arcane knowledge, what might be described as secret teachings. This mystical knowledge is found in a holy book, the *Zohar*, the book of radiance. Kabbalists generally believe in Ein Sof, which literally means 'endless,' and is also the term they use for the Creator, which can be described as the first cause or the cause of all causes. That means we can find Ein Sof present in all things in the actual world. On the other hand, all things are present in it potentially. Ein Sof, Kabbalists suggest, emanated ten Sefirot or 'vessels,' through which its actions are manifested. These Sefirot are conduits for the actions deriving from Ein Sof, and its existence is spread through them."

"I don't know what the hell you're talking about," said Weems.

"I can understand," said Dovet. "You have to be deeply immersed in it before Kabbalah starts making sense."

"Don't be put off by Weems," said Hunter. "He doesn't have a mind for abstractions. But I can follow you, so please, keep talking."

"The Kabbalists thought that if they lived a holy life and followed the teachings of the *Zohar*, the Messiah would arrive and his coming would lead to the redemption of the Jews. A great deal of Judaism is involved with the Messiah, you have to realize that. According to the Kabbalists, this mysterious Ein Sof withdrew its presence from the world. The first divine action, we are told, was this withdrawal, which created a vacuum and this emptiness enabled the world to be created. Ein Sof then sent a ray of light into this vacuum, which was channeled through the Sefirot, the vessels. But the light was so powerful that some of the vessels shattered into pieces and then returned to Ein Sof, their original source. But some became sparks that were trapped in what can be described as material existence. What Kabbalists want to do is free these sparks and return them to their original source and restore them to their divinity. They do this by living a life of holiness and by the process known as Tikkun, which means repair or mending."

"Now, if you assume that all existence is connected to the divine, everything we do, no matter how mundane, can be used as a means to discover God. Everything, no matter how small and seemingly trivial, contains the essence of divinity. Ein Sof, Kabbalists believe, exists in everything. Some Kabbalists suggest that our entire world is actually the body of God. The secret teachings revealed in the *Zohar* and other mystical writings, Kabbalists believe, are very powerful and potentially dangerous, so people must be protected from them. That's why some Kabbalists argued that people shouldn't be allowed to study the Kabbalah until they are forty years old."

"I still don't understand," said Weems.

"Let me try another way to explain things," Dovet added. "At the beginning, Kabbalists argue, everything was contained in Ein Sof and part of it. Later, Ein Sof emanated a point from itself—an emanation known as Keter, or the Crown, and from Keter, there was a second emanation, Hokhmah or Wisdom, which represented the start of revelation. This, in turn, led to a third emanation, Binah or understanding, which reveals what exists. After these three emanations, six more Sefirot appeared, representing the six different dimensions of providence—namely Gevurah or strength, Chesed or loving kindness, Tiferet or beauty, Hod or empathy, Netsah or eternity, and Yesod or foundation. Along with these six emanations, there was one more of the Sefirot that emanated, Malkhut or sovereignty. The lower Sefirot draw their power from the ones above them and they all need Ein Sof, but it doesn't need any of them."

"I'm not sure, from what you said, where these Sefirot come in," said Hunter. "If everything is part of God, why do they have a special status?"

"An excellent question," replied Dovet. "According to some Kabbalists, in the beginning, Ein Sof emanated these ten vessels or Sefirot, which were still part of Ein Sof, since everything is. Some of them have their own colors, based on their function. But the emanation from Ein Sof had no color at all, much like sunlight shining through a stained-glass window. The sunlight doesn't change its color but the viewer sees light of different colors."

"So this Ein Sof is an all-powerful presence, so it seems," said Hunter, "that manifests itself in everything. For Kabbalists, then, if I follow you correctly, everything in the world is part of God and, as such, is a means toward knowing God. Is that right?"

"Very good," said Dovet. "I've tried to make a very complicated and esoteric belief system understandable to you and, quite naturally, have left a great deal out. The other people you interview may provide more insights that will help you understand Kabbalah. All of Kabbalah can't be understood in one brief chat."

"That makes sense," replied Hunter. "So where do you fit into this research team?"

"We were just getting started, so we hadn't actually conducted any research. I'm a neurologist and Azriel wanted to find out whether the study of Kabbalah had any effect on people's brains and nervous systems. We planned on taking brain scans—that is, images of individuals before they studied Kabbalah, while they were studying Kabbalah, and after they had studied it, to see whether studying Kabbalah had any impact on various regions of the brain and whether it might have some benefits for people who had suffered minor seizures. We also hoped to take scans of students who were not studying Kabbalah as a control group to see whether we could find anything interesting.

"By understanding what's happening in the brain, we hope to learn a lot about total body health. All of medicine is a subspecialty of neurology, which is really the master discipline. It's like the Ein Sof, except instead of Sefirot we have various medical specialties, from dermatology to oncology, from proctology to surgery. The doctors who practice these specialties all think their specialties are central, the pivot around which all medicine revolves, while we neurologists *know* our specialty is of central importance. If you don't have those electrical circuits in the brain firing away, you aren't good for very much, are you? Azriel may have had an ulterior motive for inviting me to join his team. He suffers from narcolepsy and, at any moment, can fall into a deep sleep. He had spoken to me about it, though, of course, at the University of California medical center here, they have many world-class neurologists."

"How, exactly, did you become a member of this team?" asked Hunter.

"It was Azriel, of course," replied Dovet. "I had written some papers that dealt obliquely with Magnetic Resonance Imagery and religious belief and a book on Kabbalah, *NeuroKabbalah*. Azriel read some of my writings and the book and got in touch with me about joining this team. I wanted to get away from Paris and had visited San Francisco a number of times and liked the city. So I accepted Azriel's offer and came here. I have a year's appointment at the University of California Medical Center in San Francisco as a visiting professor. Our team has had meetings most mornings for the past couple of months while we plan our research. It's very interesting. Or was, before Azriel's unfortunate and untimely death."

"What was he like?" asked Hunter.

"Azriel was a brilliant physician and strategic researcher. He was a psychiatrist and had done important research on stress and anxiety. He was, for a time, at Cornell Medical Center in New York City. He got a grant and spent some time in Israel where he did some pathbreaking work on how Israelis deal with stress. You can imagine how difficult it is for most Israelis, living in a country where they are constantly under attack by suicide bomber-murderers. He did pioneering work on how Israelis function in such circumstances. He was a scholar and more interested in conducting research than in having a medical practice, though, as I understand it, he did see some patients in his earlier years here at the medical school. Researchers are animated by the notion that their contributions, their discoveries, help other doctors improve their work."

"He was invited to join the faculty at the University of California Medical School and came here a number of years ago. He obtained a large grant from some foundation to investigate the Kabbalah and how its study affected people. There's a rumor that the money originally came from Madonna. Can you imagine that? He put the team together because, in part, he was interested in Jewish mysticism and the Kabbalah and in part because he thought it would be a way to deal with mysticism in general."

"Yes, but what was he like?" asked Weems. "You've not said anything about his personality. It strikes me that his murder was probably connected more to his relationships with others on the team than his interest in this Kabbalah stuff."

"One should not speak ill of the dead," replied Dovet.

"Indulge us," Hunter said.

Dovet sighed, and shrugged his shoulders in resignation.

"How should I put this?" said Dovet. "Azriel was a complicated person. He had a wonderful sense of humor, and was very witty, but he wasn't the nicest human being in the world. That's often the case with humorous types. They've a lot of hostility and aggression in them that finds its expression in their humor. That was Freud's theory—that humor involves masked aggression. Azriel wasn't easy to get along with. He was brilliant and imaginative, but he also tended to be somewhat arrogant. When he was in a bad mood he could get quite nasty and insulting. And he liked to have his own way. He was the director of the interdisciplinary team that he assembled and, though he wasn't open about it, he always wanted things to go his way. All the time."

"If that were the case, why didn't people resign?" asked Hunter.

"It isn't easy to come to San Francisco and get established, as the other members of the team did, and then suddenly leave. After you leave, what do you do? If you've had any experience with professors, you realize that Azriel wasn't very different from most other academics. I could have resigned, since I have a position at a medical school. But the others were on leaves of absences and soft money and if they left, they'd have no income. So we all gritted our teeth for the past two months and waited for the research to begin. Then we wouldn't have these terrible meetings, that dragged on endlessly, while we worked out our research program."

"Did the other members of your team feel the same way as you did?" asked Hunter.

"I believe so," replied Dovet, "though nobody fought with Azriel at the meetings we had. But from chatting with the others, I got that feeling. Lately, he became, for some reason I can't put my finger on, hostile toward Svetalana, the Russian historian on the team. There's a rumor that she dumped him for someone else, though there are also rumors to the effect that they maintained a relationship on the sly. I think he induced her to join the team because he wanted to sleep with her. He had met her when he gave a lecture at the University of Tartu in Russia the year before. There's some question about who she really likes. She probably led Azriel along to get out of Russia. She wouldn't be the first woman to do that kind of thing to a man."

"She's the redhead, right?" said Weems.

"Yes," said Dovet. "The redhead. A very beautiful and fascinating woman, but also very difficult..." He paused for a moment. "I...I'm recently divorced and not interested in getting involved with any woman now. But if I were interested in having a relationship with a woman, I could easily be attracted to her. Very easily. In Kabbalistic thought, red represents Binah or judgment. Ironically, getting involved with Svetlana would represent a serious lack of judgment. Or maybe, and perhaps this is a better term, a lack of Chochma, wisdom."

"So you weren't—how I should I put it—'interested' 'in Svetlana?" replied Hunter.

"Not at all," said Dovet. His blinked at Hunter impassively.

"What about the other woman—the blonde?" asked Hunter.

"Krista. She's a medical sociologist from Italy. A lovely woman. Brilliant, warm, full of brio. But also a bit driven and not my type. You sense an enormous amount of energy and passion in her."

"Is it possible that she was involved with Azriel?" asked Hunter.

"You ask excellent questions," said Dovet. "As a matter of fact, there was gossip to the effect that Azriel had been sleeping with Krista and then, for some reason, abandoned her abruptly. She never said anything but I've heard that she was devastated. Why she got involved with him in the first place is difficult to say. I've heard talk that a number of years ago he prevented her from getting a chair at Yale, so you'd think she'd never have anything to do with him. In any case, it looks like he abandoned—I guess the word you Americans would use would be dumped—Krista unceremoniously a few weeks ago. He then turned his attentions toward Svetlana. But it would seem that she wasn't the least interested in him. Krista spent a lot of time with Leon Gerhard. They may have had a relationship, too. It's hard to say."

"Yes," replied Hunter. "It seems as complicated as the Kabbalah."

At this Dovet smiled.

"Nothing in the world is as complicated as the Kabbalah, or as simple, to those who are able to understand it," he replied.

"You mentioned Gerhard. What can you tell me about him. . . he is, I take it, the psychologist on the team?" asked Hunter.

"Leon Gerhard is an enigma to all of us. He always was cordial and pleasant, but I felt he was holding something back. He also has a good sense of humor. But still, something of a cold fish. From conversations we had, I had the notion—strange as it might seem—that although he's a rabbi, he doesn't believe in the existence of God. Yet, like so many people, he was fascinated by Kabbalah and by the complicated structures of thought that has been created in God's name. Some students of the Kabbalah argue that it's nothing but different names of God. Leon had a strange relationship with Azriel. He resented Azriel and claimed Azriel 'used' him, that he stole his ideas and didn't give him credit for them. But Leon also was, so the gossip goes, sexually attracted to him"

"You mean you think Leon is gay?"

"A closet homosexual," said Dovet. "But you didn't hear it from me." Dovet shook his head ruefully.

"One thing that is difficult for me to deal with as a Kabbalist," Dovet said, "is the fact that Ein Sof was present in the soul of the victim, but also is present in the soul of the murderer. The murderer had too much of what Kabbalists call Gevurah and not enough Chesed. That is, too much strength or passion and not enough loving kindness."

"I can understand that," added Hunter. "That's generally the case with premeditated murders. What did you do after your morning session broke up?" asked Hunter.

"I went to my office and searched for a book I wanted to look at," he said. "I got a phone call from Krista. In the middle of it she asked me to hold the line as somebody had come with whom she had to say a few words. I heard her talking to someone, then two or three minutes later she continued our conversation. It seems she had read an article about imaging and wanted to find out more about it. A short while later, during the middle of our conversation, there was some commotion and screaming. We hung up and I ran out into the corridor, where I discovered what had happened."

"Is there anything else you can think of that might be of interest to us?" Hunter asked.

Dovet paused for a moment, thinking things over.

"No, inspector. I've told you everything I know or that I can remember that in any way bears on this tragedy."

"I see," said Hunter. "Since we've covered things pretty well in this interview, you can go. We'll need a second one if we have more questions to ask, of course."

"Oh," said Dovet. "More than one interview? Or is interrogation a better term?"

"Whatever you wish to call it," said Hunter.

Weems poked his head out into the hall, and called down to Officer Abe Kook, one of the officers guarding the professors, "We're done with our first interview. Would you please escort Dr. Dovet back to the room with the other suspects and bring us Miss Pagetsky—the red-headed woman?"

"Suspects?" said Dovet. "We're all suspects? I find that word very disturbing, I must say."

"It happens to be the correct word," said Hunter. "There's been a murder and you and your colleagues were here when the murder took place. Unless we have reason to believe a total stranger or somebody we don't know about killed Dr. Moshe, I'm afraid you're all suspects."

At this Dovet got up. He had a grim look on his face.

"Are we done here?" Dovet said.

"Thank you," said Hunter. "We've learned a lot from this discussion." Dovet nodded tightly and left. Officer Kook escorted him back to the seminar room.

"What a messy murder this is turning out to be," said Weems. "It's hard to figure out what's going on—in Kabbalah or in the minds of the people on this team that Moshe assembled."

"Talcott—murders are always messy and complicated," said Hunter. "That's what makes them so interesting. But I'm sure we'll get to the bottom of it all sooner or later."

Sefer ha-Zohar, the Book of Splendor, Radiance, Enlightenment, has amazed and overwhelmed readers for seven centuries. The *Zohar* is the major text of Kabbalah, the Jewish mystical tradition. It's arranged in the form of a commentary on the Torah, the Five Books of Moses. It's a mosaic of Bible, midrash. . . medieval homily, fiction, and fantasy. Its central theme is the interplay of human and divine realities. Its language is a peculiar brand of Aramaic that breaks the rules of grammar and invents words. (1983:xv)

- Daniel Chanan Matt, Foreword, *Zohar: The Book of Enlightenment*

5

The Beauty Queen

"Talcott, what do you make of Professor Dovet?" asked Hunter.

"I don't know," said Weems. "I can't figure him out. He had a lot of things to tell us about the other members of the team he's on but he didn't reveal very much about himself."

"When I asked him about Professor Pagetsky, did you see how he tried to appear impassive? It was if he were trying to suppress any emotional responses to the question. I wonder how he really feels about her. Remember what we found in Moshe's journal...Moshe wrote that Dovet is crazy about Pagetsky and spends his time gazing at her, lost in his day dreams. There's reason to believe that Dovet is holding things back from us," said Hunter.

"That's probably why he was so upset when you said we might be interviewing him again," said Weems. "Suspects who are lying always are upset when they learn that there might be more than one interview."

There was a knock on the door and office Kook poked his head in.

"Professor Pagetsky is here," he said.

"Show her in," said Hunter.

With that, Svetlana Pagetsky made her grand entrance—her hips swaying, her short skirt revealing her shapely legs. She had an unpleasant, pained look on her face, as if this questioning she was to be subjected to was an irritant she wanted to put behind her as quickly as possible so she could attend to other, more important matters. Like many beautiful women, Svetlana Pagetsky was aware of her beauty and its power. She was tall and slender and wore clothes that called attention to her figure. Her long red hair framed her delicately featured face. She carried herself like a ballerina or a movie star who was used to being the center of attention whenever she walked in a room.

"How terrible all of this is," she said, in a soft voice. "Poor Azriel. Such a lovely man. To be murdered in cold blood, like this. It's truly tragic."

She paused and dabbed her eyes with a silk handkerchief with her right hand.

"I will tell you everything I know, Inspector," she added. "The murderer must be brought to justice. He couldn't have been someone in our group. It's simply impossible to think that one of us could have done such a horrible thing."

"Why do you say that?" asked Hunter.

"We're all professional people with advanced degrees, scholars with international reputations. It doesn't seem like an educated person could murder someone in cold blood. I can't believe it could be one of us, which is why I think your idea of making us remain cooped up in that room while you interview us is a mistake."

"Inspector Hunter and I have been involved in half a dozen cases investigating murders committed by professors," said Weems. "They're no different from anyone else, believe me."

"You're joking," she replied.

"But it's true," added Hunter. "Weems is right. Professors are no different from anyone else when it comes to their passions and all-consuming jealousies and hatreds, the kind that lead to murder. The only difference between scholars and other people, I've found, is that the scholars are more manipulative, more duplicitous, and plan their murders more carefully. But like all murderers, they all think they're going to get away with killing someone and not get caught. In that respect, they're like everyone else."

"How sad," she said. "You'd think that people with advanced educations would be more rational."

"Rationality flies out the window when passion walks in the room," said Hunter. "But let's get down to business, if you don't mind. Where you were educated? How did you became a member of this team?"

"I was educated at Moscow State University," she said, "and then, for my advanced degree, in what you might understand as cultural history, I went to the University of Tartu, though, to be more precise, my interest was a combination of history and semiotics—a term that probably doesn't mean anything to you. Semiotics is the science of signs and deals with how meaning is created and generated. It's really a branch of linguistics applied to cultural phenomena."

"I've been married and divorced twice. I was forced into my first marriage by my parents. I went along with it because my head was full of fantasies of romance. I was intoxicated by the image of myself in a beautiful white gown walking down the central aisle in a large church. It was when my husband and I left the church that things started going wrong, and in a short while my husband revealed himself to be an ignorant brute. That marriage didn't last long. My second marriage was a mistake that I made. I thought I'd found the perfect man, but once we were married, he turned out to be quite a different person than the one I thought I knew. He was, I discovered, a carbon copy of my first husband. So I got another quick divorce. Since then I've become much more cautious. I've been afraid that I'll make another mistake. I don't seem to have luck with husbands, and I've found, to my great pleasure, that I can actually enjoy life much better as a single woman. No cooking, no shopping, no cleaning the house, no snoring husbands. I can avoid that kind of thing. I like men but I find that I don't like husbands."

She looked away from Hunter sadly.

"Tell me, and forgive me if this question is blunt. Did you have an intimate relationship with Dr. Moshe?" asked Hunter.

Pagetsky's face took on a surprised look.

"What right do you have to ask me that kind of a question?" she exclaimed.

"Professor Pagetsky, we're investigating a brutal murder," replied Hunter. "And we want to make sure that we don't have a second murder to investigate. Whoever killed Dr. Moshe will kill again if he, or she, feels threatened."

"She? You certainly don't think a woman could have done something like this," Pagetsky replied, with a shocked expression on her face. "You can't believe that! This whole thing is becoming surreal. First you think that the murderer may be a member of the team and then you suggest the murderer could be a woman!"

"In a lot of the cases we've investigated it was a woman who was the murderer," said Weems dryly. "Women are just as capable of sticking a knife in someone's back or slipping some poison in a drink as men are. I don't know what it's like in Tartu or other parts of Russia, but here in the states there are lots of women who are killers. Our prisons are full of them."

"To return to my original question," said Hunter. "Were you having an affair with Professor Moshe?"

"An affair? Not really," said Pagetsky. "He came to give a lecture at Tartu, where we met at a party. One thing led to another and we slept together. Yes, I admit it. But I slept with him only because I knew that he represented the only hope I had of escaping from Russia and coming to the United States. He was, I should say, forceful one evening. We had been out to dinner and then had gone drinking in some bars in Tartu. These things happen. I've slept with many men, and not always for as good a reason. You probably think badly of me, but I'm not unlike many other women in this respect. You should know that. But we didn't have an affair, as you would call it. Not by any means. And when I got here I told Azriel that I wouldn't be carrying on with him the way I did in Tartu. I made that clear to him before I accepted a position on his research team."

"I see," said Hunter. "And what were you going to contribute to this team? How does semiotics and history fit in?"

"You have to realize that the Kabbalah, whatever else it might be, is an extremely elaborate system of signs. All those Sefirot and the various paths between and among them—they make up a fascinating symbology, whose meaning is very elusive. And there are countless other diagrams and mystical drawings made by Kabbalists. As a historian and semiotician, tracing the development of the Kabbalah movement and the exotic symbolization system integrated into it is a formidable challenge. The term 'Kabbalah' means traditional teachings in Hebrew, but its teachings are anything but traditional, based, as they are, on the ideas of a number of mystical thinkers. Its followers used to be known as the 'hochmah nistarah,' or searchers after hidden wisdom. An ingenious acrostic also led to them being called 'yorde hen' or connoisseurs of divine grace."

"The goal of the kabbalists is similar to that of other Jewish mystical traditions—to hasten the coming of the Messiah. Kabbalistic thought is divided into two streams. One involves our lives in the everyday world which, they believe, have sprung out of the essence of God—the Kabbalah Iyunith. The other involves investigating mystical words and names, which allegedly have great powers. Many kabbalists believe that their investigations into the divine essence and the mysterium of language and signs imitates that of God, who they believe has a school of study in heaven. This divine wisdom, it is held, was transmitted directly to the great figures of the Torah, such as Adam, Moses, David and Solomon. It was only when Simeon ben Yohai, who was alive at the time of the destruction of the Second Temple, revealed this secret knowledge that we learned of it. But some Kabbalists believe its esoteric teachings date back a great deal earlier, and are actually derived from the beliefs of Jewish people in ancient times, who felt very close to the divine presence and believed that God took a personal interest, so to speak, in everything they did."

"Let me get this straight," said Weems. "Are you saying that for the Kabbalists, God is like a professor teaching some kind of an advanced course in divine Kabbalistic thought in heaven, and that modern Kabbalists are imitating him?"

"For some Kabbalists," replied Pagetsky. "It's impossible to say that all Kabbalists believe anything—aside from the existence of God, that is. And maybe not even that."

"So, for Kabbalists God is a professor," added Hunter. "That may help explain why professors think so highly of themselves. They all have a touch of the Kabbalist sense of having a kind of divine knowledge. Or of being gods?"

Pagetsky smiled.

"Perhaps we do," she replied. "You need to have courage to attack conventional knowledge. And maybe many professors feel they have special insights and, after years of study, perhaps even what might be called wisdom. Like the Kabbalists. The roots of Kabbalistic thought go deep in Jewish history, and it can be argued that there were a number of mystical theorists and theories that were popular over the millenia. But it was when the *Sefer Ha-Zohar,* the book of splendor—otherwise known as the *Zohar*, was written, that the different strands of Jewish mystical thought came together and into focus. Originally it was thought that Simeon ben Yohai wrote the book in the Second Century, but it's now known that it was written in the Thirteenth Century by the mystic Moses de Leon. He had claimed to have transcribed the *Zohar* from a manuscript that rabbi ben Yohai had written or compiled a thousand years earlier, to escape criticism and help sell copies of his book. But de Leon's wife admitted that he wrote the book, that it came out of his head, so to speak.

"The Jews seized upon the *Zohar* and Kabbalistic mysticism as a means of finding solace, after their expulsion from Spain and in the middle of the Sixteenth Century, around 1550, a number of Jewish mystics in Israel such as Isaac Luria and Moses Cordovero got together and speculated about the *Zohar*. They believed that this mystical god-force, Ein Sof, manifested his existence by means of the ten Sefirot, which are divine emanations that flow from him and all partake of his perfection. There was an archetypal man, Adam Kadmon, who was part of the Malkut or tenth emanation, representing kingdom. What Kabbalists do is search for signs of God hidden in every aspect of life, signs that are not recognized by those without familiarity with the secret knowledge of the Kabbalists."

"Isaac Luria was of particular interest. He invented any number of supposedly magical amulets, esoteric manipulations of words, and strange practices that Jews of his time thought had great powers to ward off evil. He left no writings but his teachings were recorded by a disciple named Chaim Vital and formed a book, *Etz Hayim*, or *The Tree of Life*. If you look at the manuscripts of these ancient Kabbalists, you find all kinds of fantastic and remarkable diagrams and drawings and, among other things, it is those fantastic images that I had planned on decoding. Before Azriel was murdered, that is. It is, come to think of it, as if some evil force doesn't want the secrets of the Kabbalah to be revealed and is intervening to prevent us from doing so."

She gave a deep sigh.

"Anyway, I thought I'd finally rescued myself and escaped from that prison that is Russia...I thought I had finally found a path to a decent future. During my year here I hoped to find a position in America or some European institution...now, suddenly, Azriel's death has ruined all that. I suppose I'm being terribly selfish, and thinking too much about myself."

She bit her lip, and began crying. Shakily, she held her handkerchief to her eyes. "I'm sorry, I'm feeling a bit overwhelmed," she said.

"Your feelings are perfectly natural," said Hunter, softly. "When people become involved in murder cases, they suddenly sense that they are terribly vulnerable and become frightened. It happens all the time."

"Yes, yes...I can see that," she said, in a weak voice.

"What about the other members of the team? What can you tell us about them? For example, what's interesting to know about Jean-Pascal Dovet?" asked Weems.

Svetlana looked at Weems pensively.

"Poor Jean-Pascal. I'm afraid, for some reason that I can't fathom, he's become hostile to me in a most irrational way. Not that he's ever said anything or done anything that would reveal that, but I get the sense when I talk to him that he despises me. And I can't figure out why. He's perfectly cordial, mind you. But underneath I sense what might be described as hatred, even loathing. Perhaps I remind him of his former wife. He's recently divorced, you know. It may be that he's attracted to me but since he feels the situation is hopeless and so has turned against me."

"And what was he doing on the team?" asked Hunter.

"He's a physician—a neurologist. He was interested in brain waves of Kabbalists. He wanted to record their brain waves when they were involved with their Kabbalistic practices and to compare the brains of Kabbalists with non-Kabbalistic Jews and, if I remember things correctly, with gentiles. To my way of thinking Jean-Pascal's project was terribly far-fetched, but of course I speak as a historian and semiotician and don't know that much about medicine. He was obsessed with brain waves and squiggles on charts that he made from the electronic activity of people's brains. How bizarre; and he wrote a book *NeuroKabbalah* that attracted a lot of attention. I think it went to his head, to tell you the truth. I looked at it but it was full of medical terminology that didn't make sense to me."

"Did he have the same strong feelings towards others in the team? What about the blonde woman? Did he hate all women or just you?"

"Krista is a lovely woman. She's kind, gentle, and quite brilliant. A truly beautiful soul," said Svetalana. As she did, the muscles of her face relaxed and, for a brief instant, her face glowed. "No," she continued, "I think Jean-Pascal reserved his enmity for me. I think he's very fond of Krista, as a matter of fact. They often had lunch together. I used to join them from time to time, when I wasn't occupied with my research."

"What's she doing on the team?" asked Weems. "I'm trying to figure out how this interdisciplinary business works. Sounds like a lot of nonsense to me."

"She's a sociologist who's interested in religion. She's written some truly important, pioneering books. Her most famous one is called *The Kabbalah Brotherhood: A Sociological Inquiry.* She's interested in what kind of Jews, and non-Jews as well—since the Kabbalah has become popular and trendy of late—become attracted to Kabbalah and why it intrigues them so much. Like many things in Judaism, the group is important in Kabbalistic practice, and she wants to know how these groups function and what role they play in the lives of Kabbalists."

"What about the English psychologist, Leon Gerhard? What role did he play in this team?" asked Hunter.

"Leon, you should know, is a Rabbi, but more importantly, for this project, he's a psychologist," she replied. "He was brought in to study the psychological makeup of Kabbalists. But also because he is a scholar of the Kabbalah and could help the team understand its basic principles, when that was necessary."

"So you had a neurologist, a psychologist, a historian, a sociologist, and a psychiatrist on this team that Moshe assembled," said Hunter. "And you were all to study, in one respect or another, the way the Kabbalah affected people—psychologically, physically and any other way you could devise. Is that correct?"

"Yes," said Pagetsky. "In universities nowadays it's quite common to put together this kind of a team, since we recognize now that there are many different facets to be studied in phenomena like Kabbalism and numerous other topics. The disciplines are all merging together now. For example, we have psychologists studying sociological phenomena and sociologists studying psychological phenomena, which explains why you can find courses in social psychology in both sociology and psychology departments in many universities. Leon Gerhard has an international reputation and Moshe was very happy and suprised that he joined the team."

"Surprised?" asked Hunter. "Why was he surprised?"

"There was, for a long time, bad blood between them," she replied. "Leon claimed that Azriel stole some of his ideas in a book he wrote on the Kabbalah—*The Mind of the Mystic*. I take it that they had been good friends, and then there was a falling out. These things happen. Leon, you'll find, is a very interesting man. Very good looking, sophisticated, charming, often quite amusing, and a world class scholar. He graduated first in his class at Cambridge and he ended up, after a few years in a provincial university in England, with a chair in psychology at Berkeley."

"I see," said Hunter.

"You said he was good looking," said Weems. "Are we to infer that you might have been interested in him?"

At this Pagetsky laughed.

"Good looking, indeed. Quite handsome, as a matter of fact. But, alas, not the kind of man who likes women like me, or any women. One reason he wanted to come to San Francisco to teach and conduct research is the fact that this city has a certain reputation."

"Tell me, what did you do after the morning meeting broke up?" asked Hunter.

"I went to my office to make some phone calls. I was waiting to go to lunch with Krista. She said she had something to do and it would be only a few minutes. We were going to some new Italian restaurant, Bardolino's, that she'd heard good things about."

"I see," said Hunter. "Is there anything else you think might be important to tell us?""

Pagetsky paused for a moment, thinking.

"No, inspector. I think I've told you everything," she replied.

"Okay," said Hunter. "If there's nothing else you can think of to tell us at this time, I'll have an officer bring you back to the room where your colleagues are waiting to be interviewed. We may want to talk with you again, later, after we've interviewed the other suspects."

"Suspects?" she exclaimed. "That word has an ominous ring."

"Perhaps," said Hunter. "But victim has an even more ominous ring, and so does murder. Someone has been murdered, and it looks like a member of your team was the killer."

"Yes. . . yes, you're right," she said. She now had a grim, troubled look on her face. "I hadn't thought of it that way. So I'm a suspect, too."

"I'm afraid you are," said Hunter.

"Well," she replied, "people have said all kinds of terrible things about me over the years—that I'm a sexual predator, a nymphomaniac, a gold-digger, a charlatan. Why not add murderer to the list?"

At that she laughed.

"The Kabbalah," she added. "I thought it was going to liberate me, to help me find a new life. And now it seems like a heavy burden weighing me down, crushing me underneath it. The ten Sefirot—the magical manifestations of Ein Sof—and the esoteric teachings of Moses de Leon and Moses Cordovero and all the others. Look what they've accomplished for me. The light of the Kabbalah has brought me nothing but pain and anguish. Well, sometimes you make a mistake and take a wrong turn on the road to wherever you're going, or think you were going. But this isn't the end. There's still hope for the future. That's one of the things the Kabbalah teaches. If I could survive those terrible winters in Tartu and two horrible husbands, I can survive this, too."

Hunter called down the hallway and Officer Kook appeared.

"Please escort Professor Pagetsky back to the room where her colleagues are located. And then, in ten minutes, bring us Professor Gerhard," Hunter said. "Talcott and I want to talk about things for a few minutes before we see the next suspect."

Svetlana Pagetsky got up and started walking towards the door.

"I hope you catch the murderer, and soon. Azriel wasn't always the nicest person in the world, but he didn't deserve a knife in his back."

If I told them my secret, that I am writing from my own mind, they would pay no attention to my words, and they would pay nothing for them. They would say: "He is inventing them out of his imagination." But now that they hear that I am copying from *The Book of Zohar* composed by Rabbi Shim'on son of Yohai through the Holy Spirit, they buy these words at a high price. (1983:4)

- Moses de Leon, Introduction to *Zohar: The Book of Enlightenment*, Transl. Daniel Chanan Matt.

6

Azriel Moshe's Journal

AZRIEL MOSHE KEPT
A JOURNAL

When she had left the room, Hunter picked up Moshe's journal and started thumbing through it.

"I wonder what he says about Pagetsky," he said.

Weems nodded. "I'm going to get a cup of coffee. Want anything?"

Hunter shook his head. Weems left, leaving the door slightly ajar. Hunter began to thumb through Moshe's journal, looking for clues. After a moment he paused, and began reading.

"Here's something strange," thought Hunter. "He's writing about his high school teachers."

I got a call from Dave Goldberg at Harvard. He wants me to give a lecture to one of his classes in a couple of weeks. I've not been to Boston in quite a while...but going back and landing at Logan airport in Boston always reminds me of my days at Central Memorial High School many years ago. I had what could be best described as an excellent Catholic education there. This was all the more remarkable since it was a public high school, run by the city of Boston, and I am Jewish. Most of my teachers were Catholic (and many of them Irish Catholics) and from Catholic universities like Holy Cross and Boston College. Memorial was an ugly, square monolith that was about ten blocks from where I lived.

I still remember a number of my teachers. They can best described as a congress of zanies, one crazier and more eccentric than the next. It may be that teaching high school students does that to people, though in those days students seemed to be much more motivated and we had fewer distractions. Let me start with 'Preacher' Ahearn. 'Preacher' Ahearn (what was his first name?) was a dour, very religious man, who was my geometry teacher. He had jet black hair that he plastered down on his head, with a part in the middle. He had ten children. What was most bizarre was that he had all his students pray before taking exams that they would do well on them. I can remember praying, as hard as I could, that I would ace some plane geometry quiz.

'Dear God: let me remember that a straight line is the shortest distance between two points,' I would pray.

Now that I think about it, I carried this habit with me all through high school and even into my first year of college at Harvard. There, one morning, as I was praying before some exam I suddenly realized what was happening. 'What the hell am I doing?' I asked myself? And that was the end of my pre-exam praying. Nowadays, in an age that is interested in meditation and similar things, we might take more kindly to the notion of clearing one's head before undertaking some task, but the prayers I learned from Preacher Ahearn all had to do with good grades and God's mercy...these prayers were far removed from meditation or the Kabbalah.

One of my English teachers, Mr. Gemmet, was called 'the G-Man.' That was because, in the middle of a sentence he would suddenly disappear. He would run out of the classroom and dash into a bathroom to see whether anyone was smoking. The G-Man also worked as a painter during the summer, and used to talk about how he lugged huge forty-foot ladders around. He was balding, had gray hair and gray eyes, if I remember correctly.

I learned I was an iconoclast from Mr. Delahany, my French teacher. He always had the smell of menthol cough drops on his breath. This was, we all assumed, to hide the smell of alcohol. His face was pink and blotched and we all assumed that he was a hard drinker. He said to me once, 'You're an iconoclast.' I think I was in the eleventh grade. I went home, looked the word up, and decided it fit. So when I was as young as sixteen, I was already 'at war' with conventions and with commonly accepted notions of what makes the world go around.

Mr. O'Hanlon, the 'Boss' as he was known, was head of the 'Patrol,' a group of exemplary students who patrolled the corridors, keeping order and engaged in a war to the death with student smokers. He had confiscated a number of weapons that students had brought to school over the years: baseball bats, pool cues, slingshots, and so on. He taught Civics and I can remember his tests very well. He would have us memorize the first paragraph of the Declaration of Independence and his examinations would be as follows: 1. What is the third word after the fourth 'and'? 2. What is the fifth word after the second 'the'? 3. What is the fourth word after 'truths'?

He built a platform under his desk that was about eighteen inches high so he could peer down on his students as they listened to his lectures and wrote their examinations, reciting the Declaration of Independence to themselves and trying to figure out what the fourth word after the third 'and' in that text might be?

Hunter shook his head, and scanned on a few more pages.

Weems returned with a cup of coffee. "Find anything?"

"Not yet. I can't find anything on Pagetsky, but there's lots of mumbo-jumbo in here about this Ein Sof and the ten emanations and some curious diagrams with Hebrew letters and words that he pasted in the book. Look at this one, Talcott. It's very strange." He showed the image to Weems, who shook his head in bewilderment.

"He describes this as a poem representing some kind of a magical wheel of light. These Kabbalists are big on light. But why? Maybe we should ask Gerhard about it, when we interview him," said Hunter. "I'm sure this diagram has some hidden meaning."

He continued to thumb through the journal.

"There are lots of other obscure diagrams in this journal," Hunter said. "These Kabbalists love to make really mysterious diagrams. No doubt about that."

"Look at this one," he added, and pointed to another figure. "It has a Hebrew letter in it and looks like a labyrinth of some kind. Really bizarre stuff. Maybe a labyrinth is an apt a metaphor for this investigation. For the moment, we're wandering around in the bushes and can't see what's really going on."

The Image of the Labyrinth

He flipped some more pages.

"Here's something really interesting," Hunter said. "I found something about Pagetsky. Let me read it to you."

Svetlana told me she loves me and wants to marry me. But I can't believe her. I can't believe a word she says. I suspect she wants to find a way to stay in America. We haven't had sex since those wild evenings in Russia, when we both drank too much Vodka, though heaven knows I've tried to lure her into bed since she joined our team. It's as if she finds sex with me repugnant. Or maybe sex with men repugnant? She talks endlessly about Krista and may be involved with her, though Krista seems to be interested in Leon.

Krista is angry with me for, as she put it, 'abandoning' her, but she'll get over it. I actually think she wanted to break up with me—probably because of Leon. Krista is very guarded, but I can sense that she's attracted to him, just as I can sense that he really isn't interested in her. She's actually cold and very calculating, when you think about it. Who he's interested in is beyond me. Maybe Svetlana and Leon have something going? He's young and good looking. Maybe life as the wife of a Cambridge grad is more interesting to her than finding a way to stay in America. Nothing involving my colleagues would surprise me. They all seem to have secret lives that they keep hidden from me, just as Ein Sof also is hidden from me and everyone else, though, at least, there are the ten Sefirot, which show how he manifests his presence in the world. And, of course, there is the Zohar. I've started watching my colleagues carefully and I'm sure I'll eventually get to the bottom of things.

Meanwhile, my health is not good. I don't seem to have the energy I used to have and wonder whether God will give me the strength to fathom this most marvelous of his mysteries, his existence as Ein Sof and the secrets of his ten Sefirot. The relationships of the Sefirot with one another are even more mysterious and difficult to fathom than the relationships of my colleagues with one another.

With luck, we will soon begin our research and if everything goes as it should, in six months or so we will know a great deal more about the Zohar, the psychological appeals of Kabbalism, the kind of people to whom it's attractive, and maybe we'll even be able to fathom, somehow, some of its mysteries, though people

51

have been trying to do so for hundreds, if not thousands, of years.
Maybe some of the 600,000 faces of God will be revealed to us?
Maybe the 620 names of God will be discovered?

"So, Talcott, what do you make of that?" asked Hunter. "It seems that we've got a collection of really unusual individuals on this team and that their relationships are quite convoluted. It looks like Svetlana may be a bisexual? Or perhaps even a lesbian, though that seems a bit far-fetched since she's been married twice. But married women do become one of the sisters, don't they? Just like some married men end up gay."

"Whatever she may be, I'd say she's a very determined and manipulative woman," said Weems. "She's very beautiful and knows how to use her looks for her own purposes. Women like that are always dangerous. She's a gorgeous dame, but there's something about her that's scary. That's the impression I got from our little talk. Those fake tears and all that. I imagine she's capable of anything."

"Even murder?" asked Hunter.

"Most certainly," replied Weems. "I don't think she's the type to let anything stand in the way of getting whatever she wants out of life. I wouldn't want to cross her. Not at all."

"That's interesting," said Hunter, "because I got the same feeling, more or less. From what she told us, I get the notion that she gets emotionally involved with people, perhaps deeply, but then gets bored with them and drops them when she's tired of them. She seems to have been involved sexually with Moshe for a while, which gave her a ticket to San Francisco and a job. Then she left him—perhaps for Dovet, who seems to be batty about her, and then it looks like she dumped him for Gerhard. Or maybe someone else?"

"Someone else not on the team?" asked Weems. "Or someone we don't know about? Because if it's someone on the team, that leaves the Italian blonde, Krista. And that would mean that Svetlana swings both ways."

"I don't know who to believe," said Hunter. "What's really troubling is that, for the moment, I can't find a motive. I don't see why someone felt it necessary to kill Moshe."

"Nowadays, one doesn't seem to need much of a motive to kill someone," replied Weems. "Besides, we're dealing with a bunch of thoroughbreds and they're notorious for being touchy. I don't think it would take very much to set off one of the members of the team. And I'll bet that sex is what's behind the murder. If it isn't money, it's usually sex."

"We'll probably find out what the motivation was by the time we've finished with our interrogations," said Hunter. "Which makes me think, since we're interested in motivation, it's time for us to talk with the man who may be, or have been, the object of Svetlana's affections, namely Leon Gerhard. We haven't heard that much about him so far, have we? That's kind of interesting."

Sabbatianism is Jewish mysticism driven to the utmost limits. Practically, it sought to translate mystic doctrine and mystic yearnings into the actual implementation of a program of immediate redemption. Theologically, it was prepared to open up wide spaces for the expression of the irrational and encourage a radically antinomian disruption of Jewish tradition in the name of tradition. The whole Sabbatian romance with the abyss is something that must have struck a chord in Scholem's modernist imagination, he being an intellectual who had come of age at a time of breakdown of old values, when speculative thought, literature, and the other arts were exploring the human vocation for chaos and the signs of imminent apocalypse. Scholem's larger revisionist project is, of course, to move the mystics from the margins to the center of Jewish history, to show Jews not only as reasonable and keenly analytic expounders of the Law, but also as ecstatics, ascetics, theosophists, enthusiasts, apocalyptic extremists and magicians.

- Robert Alter, Foreword, Gershom Scholem, *Major Trends in Jewish Mysticism*

7

The Rabbi

FREUD'S VIEW AND KABBALISM ARE MORE OR LESS THE SAME

Officer Kook delivered Leon Gerhard to the interrogation room after he brought Svetlana Pagetsky back to the seminar room. Gerhard was tall and slim, with wavy brown hair. He was very good looking—he had the looks of a movie star, something like Cary Grant in his younger days. Gerhard had a grim and sad expression on his face. He spoke with the received pronunciation of well-educated upper-class people from the United Kingdom.

"What a horrible day," he said after he had seated himself. "I've seen many dead people but I've never seen anyone who had been murdered."

"How come you've been involved with so many dead people?" asked Weems.

"I'm a professor," Gerhard replied, "but I'm also a rabbi, and we are often called upon to officiate at funerals. I became a professor because I don't like dealing with the kinds of things you have to deal with when you have a congregation. A few years of that kind of work—dealing with cliques and elements in a congregation that despise one another, or, in some cases, also despised me—believe me, it wasn't fun. Church politics are the same. One can't help but wonder why there aren't more murders in churches and synagogues and mosques as well. In any case, my interest in psychology led me away from being a rabbi for a congregation. I have a doctorate in psychology from Cambridge, so I had my choice of paths to take. And the path I took brought me, after a few years in England, to a professorship here at the University of California, though, interestingly enough, I think it was my fascination with the Kabbalah that led me to become a psychologist."

"How so?" asked Hunter.

"Kabbalistic thought maintains that everything in the universe is a manifestation of God's will. It suggests that behind every act we do or object we see there is a secret and hidden meaning or dimension that only those who have learned certain esoteric knowledge can understand. This perspective on things is the same as that of Freud, for example, who suggested there is an unconscious element to the human psyche that the ordinary person cannot access, and that this unconscious, in mysterious ways, shapes our behavior. The basic metaphor is an iceberg. What we can see above the water represents human consciousness. We can make out part of the iceberg in the area below the water, for six feet or so, and this Freud called the preconscious. It's accessible to us. But below this area, in the dark, there is most of the iceberg and we are unable to see it. This is the unconscious, and it's not accessible to people, though with the help of psychologists, some of it can be ascertained."

"The point of view of Freud and the Kabbalists is the same, for all practical purposes," he added. "Everything we do, from a psychoanalytic perspective, is a combination of conscious intentions and unconscious imperatives. What makes things interesting is that the unconscious imperatives shape our conscious intentions, so we have the illusion that we are making up our own minds about certain things we do, whereas in reality they are shaped by the unconscious. Now, if you translate this perspective on things from the human psyche to the human soul, you find yourself with mysticism, and, for the Jews, the Kabbalah. It isn't the only mystical thread in Judaism but it's probably the most important form of Jewish mysticism.

"The central book of the Kabbalah is a really gigantic volume, of many thousand pages called the *Zohar*. It was written, we now know, around 1280 over the course of a number of years by a Spanish Jew, a mystic named Moses de Leon. Some of it seems to be the result of what we now call 'automatic writing' in which a writer writes down, without stopping for a moment to think, whatever comes into his head. He claimed to be copying an ancient text written by Rabbi Simeon bar Yohai, who was a disciple of one of Judaism's greatest rabbis, Rabbi Akiba, of blessed memory. In reality, we know that de Leon spun the *Zohar* out of some combination of his background in mystical Jewish thought, other mystical works, and a fertile imagination."

"Is this sort of like the Book of Mormon?" asked Weems.

Gerhard laughed.

"An apt comparison," he said. "There are many religions that are based on what is alleged to be a divinely inspired book—the case of the Mormons is one example, and so is the Torah, the New Testament for Christians, and, for Muslims, the Koran. Books can have an enormous impact—something we tend to forget about nowadays due to our fascination with television and film and other kinds of popular culture. You can say that half a dozen or so books have shaped religious consciousness over the millenia and, in so doing, have shaped our consciousness and the world order."

"So you read the book and do what it says," said Weems. "That seems simple enough. But what do you do when the books of major religions contradict one another? And they do, don't they? Don't the Christians claim to have supplanted the Jews, who didn't recognize Christ, and don't the Muslims claim to have supplanted the Christians, who don't recognize Mohammed?"

"You raise interesting questions," said Gerhard. "But it isn't quite as simple as that. One thing you have to realize is that language is often very ambiguous... and it isn't always possible to be certain what something in the Torah or the *Zohar* means. Or even the Constitution, written just a few hundred years ago. We can never be sure what the words in a book—and the term we use in the academy for these religious works or any work, is 'texts'—we can never be sure what they mean. The words are frequently ambiguous and there are gaps that readers often have to supply to make sense of things because the writing is often elliptical. In addition, texts are often influenced, directly or indirectly, by other texts—a concept known as 'intertextuality.' So there's no such thing, I would argue, as one, true, obvious, literal meaning to any text. In Judaism, there is a term for the interpretations that countless generations of rabbis and scholars have made of the Torah. The term is 'midrash.' So, in the final analysis, with the Torah, the *Zohar*, or any text, you find people—in our case rabbis—interpreting these texts and these interpretations are shaped by the nature of the text and by the cultural codes that shape the thinking of the people doing the interpreting."

"I hate to say this," said Hunter, "But your statement reminds me of the kind of thinking we came up against when we were involved with a murder of a postmodernist professor a few years ago. If I remember correctly, the postmodernists also used the term intertextuality. And so did some literary criticism types we were involved with, too. They all had different interpretations of *Hamlet*. Are they all offshoots, in some strange, way of the Kabbalistic frame of mind?"

"So, we've got Freudians and literary theorists and postmodernists all linked, indirectly, to Kabbalah here. Or the perspective Kabbalists have on things. That's what you're suggesting," said Gerhard. "The notion isn't as far-fetched as you might imagine. It's possible to argue that there's an infinite kind of regression that can be made as we find modern texts intertextually related to older ones that are related to still older ones, ad infinitum. There is some question about whether the kind of interpretation I'm talking about is correct; there are some scholars who argue that the words and meaning of a text are obvious and easy to understand. Read the Bible and do what it says. But what does it say? In the case of the Torah, the first five books of the Old Testament, rabbis and other Jewish thinkers have pored over every word and phrase in it and come up with countless different interpretations.

"That's where the line between modernists and fundamentalists is drawn. Fundamentalists believe it's all very simple—just take everything you read in a text, like the Bible, literally. Modernists argue that in the final analysis, you have to interpret everything. And interpretations are based on all kinds of different matters, such as the nature of the writing in the text, the gaps in it, and the consciousness of those making the interpretations."

"So—who's right?" asked Hunter.

"Each of us thinks that we're right and everyone else—or, more precisely, anyone who disagrees with us—is wrong," replied Gerhard. "That's what makes it so interesting. But I should point out that all interpretations are not equally valid. Some interpretations— which explain more things, which have greater depth, which connect in more interesting ways to previous passages in the Torah— are better than others. You have to realize that all texts are enormously complicated, even though they may seem quite straightforward and easy to understand. The Torah is full of stories, and we now realize that narratives work in strange and unexplainable ways. The same applies to the *Zohar*, which is a gigantic work full of all kinds of different genres—poems, narratives, automatic writing, explications—you name it."

"And what role were you supposed to play in this team? Were you going to psychoanalyze Kabbalists?" Hunter asked.

"I brought two things to the team," Gerhard replied. "First, I'm a psychologist and can apply the insights I've gained from my study of the human psyche to the investigations of Kabbalism that we had planned. And secondly, I'm a rabbi, and thus brought another thing to the team—namely, my knowledge of Judaism and my training in ways of analyzing the Torah and other sacred Jewish texts. I ought to say, also, that I find the Kabbalah extremely interesting and attractive. It speaks to a need people have for an emotional relationship with the divine, for a sense of mystery and magic, as contrasted with the rational approach you find in many religions nowadays."

"But what, precisely, were you going to do?" asked Hunter. "I'm aware of your qualifications, but what did you plan to investigate and how were you going to do it?"

"I see what you want to know," said Gerhard. "But it's difficult to tell you, because we were still at the preliminary stages of our research. Jean-Pascal is a neurologist and had a pretty good idea about what he wanted to do. He wanted to make brain scans of Kabbalists to see which areas of their brains were being used during Kabbalistic practices and also to see whether the brains of Kabbalists were different from the brains of other Jews. My task, in rough terms, was to conduct in-depth interviews with Kabbalists and see if there is some kind of a psychological profile that can be made of Kabbalists. That is, I wanted to learn something about their motivations, their personality traits, their make-up. For example, is there an obsessive-compulsive element to their character? Is there a paranoid element in their psyches? It's an interesting question—how do you explain the mindset of the mystic? And what are the roots of their behavior? What motivates them?"

"Okay. Now I understand what you were going to do," said Hunter. "In a sense, what you had planned to do is very similar to what we do when we investigate a murder. We're interested in motivation, too. And, like the Kabbalists, we investigate the reality hiding behind the commonplace, the ordinary, and especially the signs that mislead those who don't understand how the minds of murderers work."

"From what you say," said Gerhard, "I'd say you have the makings of a first-rate Kabbalist. When you assume that nothing is as it seems, that there are certain mysterious and hidden realities behind the commonplace, you are beginning to have the mind of the mystic, though you're approach is based on an assumption of rationality in human beings and the need to understand the motivations of people."

"Speaking of motivations, do you have any notion about who might have wanted to kill Professor Moshe, and why they might have wished to do so?"

Gerhard laughed.

"You must forgive me if I seem callous and unsympathetic," he said, "but everyone on this team had good reason to kill Azriel. We all might have come from different disciplines, but we were all united in one respect—everyone on the team hated Azriel, and some members of this team, perhaps every member of the team, despised him. Underneath the kindly and gentle persona that was his public face, he was, you have to realize, a terrible person—mean, vindictive, unscrupulous and dishonest. I would imagine that most of the members of the team didn't realize how despicable and depraved he was, and were flattered when he invited them to join his research team and spend some time in San Francisco. It didn't take long, however, for him to reveal himself to others, for his duplicitous personality to manifest itself, for his temper to flare. In our tradition, we're told not to speak ill of anyone—especially the dead. But Azriel was a monster! A brilliant monster, but a monster, nevertheless, and I'm afraid I can't be honest and truthful in this interrogation and not tell the truth about Azriel."

"Why did you join his team?" asked Weems. "You knew what he was like. And you're a professor here at the university. What did you have to gain? Why did you subject yourself to all this misery if you didn't have to?"

"That's an excellent question. The topic was so interesting that I couldn't help myself. I have an affinity for the Kabbalah. And I thought I could handle Azriel. I knew what kind of person he was and thought that knowledge would enable me to deal with him, and, I hoped, protect other members of the team. I was right, up to a point. But I couldn't forget how he had stolen my ideas. We were collaborating on a project a number of years ago. Unbeknownst to me, Azriel took my ideas and rushed them into print. As a result of this so-called 'seminal' book he became a world renowned figure, leaving me in the shadows, so to speak, unknown, unrecognized and very bitter. Nor could I stomach the way he conducted the meetings: his sarcastic remarks, his condescending tone. It wasn't easy restraining myself, I must admit. But I managed to keep control of my feelings. Taking Valium helped."

Gerhard was perspiring now. He took out a handkerchief and wiped his brow.

"You must forgive me," he said. "I can't help but get emotional when I talk about Azriel. I can't seem to let go of my grievances. Perhaps the others you've interrogated have expressed similar views?"

"We're getting lots of different pictures of Professor Moshe," replied Hunter, "and of the Kabbalah and the Kabbalists. We're learning a great deal. Tell me, what were his relations with Svetlana Pagetsky like? Did he put her on the team because she's a beautiful woman or because she's a topnotch scholar? Or both? The other woman on the team, Professor Scelba, she's also a very good looking women. Was there anything going on between Moshe and Pagetsky or Moshe and Scelba that I should know about?"

"You won't be surprised, I imagine, if I add to my list of terrible things about Azriel the fact that he was a sexual predator. He was sleeping with Krista and then, without so much as a second thought, dumped her to pursue Svetlana. I take it she had slept with him in Tartu, when he went to give some lectures there. And he hoped to return to bed with her here in San Francisco, but she had other things in mind. She's a calculating woman and only used Azriel for her own purposes. Serves him right. I imagine she saw through him right away but was desperate to escape from Russia, especially if she could end up in San Francisco. She'd been here for conferences from time to time and really wanted to come back. Full of her kind of people."

"What do you mean by that?" asked Hunter.

"Didn't she tell you when you talked with her? Svetlana is a lesbian. She thought she was straight when she was young and married and divorced two men, but she's really one of the sisters of Lesbos. So San Francisco is her kind of city. But she didn't have to go looking around for a partner when she found one right on the team."

"You mean Krista Scelba?" asked Hunter. "She's the only other woman on the team. Is she a lesbian also?"

"It's sad, and even a bit ironic. Svetlana's never told Krista and never even showed her hand, but I've watched her carefully and its pretty obvious to me that Svetlana's in love with Krista. But Krista isn't gay."

"This case is getting crazier and crazier by the minute," said Weems. "You're telling us that this beautiful woman, who has been married and divorced twice, who's certainly slept with Moshe, and who's the object of Jean-Pascal Dovet's passion, is gay. It seems a bit far-fetched to me. I take it that she's not come out about her lesbianism and is still in the closet."

"Yes, that's true," said Gerhard. "But she's not the only person on the team keeping secrets."

"Who else has a secret we should know about?" asked Hunter.

"I'll tell you one more that you'll find interesting, no doubt. It further complicates things, both for you and for me."

"What's that?" asked Hunter. "This case is already complicated enough, but I want to know what this secret is."

"Krista Scelba is in love with me." said Gerhard.

"And how do you feel about her?" asked Hunter.

"She's a wonderful person but not my type—not at all, I'm afraid," replied Gerhard.

"If you've no more secrets to tell us, you can return to your colleagues," said Hunter. "I'm sure they've had a lot to say to one another about everything that's transpired today."

"Fortunately," replied Gerhard, "character assassination isn't a crime." Gerard began chuckling to himself as Hunter called Officer Kook to lead him away.

Petichta: The *Zohar* is a work of Midrash, [that is, an] imaginative interpretation of the Bible. This text, like many others in the *Zohar*, is a particular form of Midrash, a kind of sermon, called a "petichta," an "opening". When the *Zohar* says that Rabbi Chizkiya (or Rabbi El'azar) "opened," it means that he began a **petichta**. At the same time, we can understand it to mean that he "opened" the hidden meanings of the verses he quotes from the Bible...

Rabbi Chizkiyah (in some manuscripts Rabbi El'azar) opened:

It's written
"Like a rose among the thorns."
Song of Songs 2:2
Who is the rose?
The rose is the Community of Israel,
because there is a rose and there is a rose.
Just as the rose, who is among the thorns, has in her
      red and white,
so the Community of Israel has in her
justice and compassion.
Just as the rose has in her thirteen leaves (petals),
so the Community of Israel has in her thirteen measures of compassion,
which surround her from all sides.

  - www.kolen.org/*Zohar*/mod1.1.html, accessed 8/12/2003

8

Solomon Hunter and Talcott Weems Speculate

"What do you make of our psychologist-rabbi?" Hunter asked? "He's another enigmatic figure in this story."

"Too much intellect and not enough heart, or soul," replied Weems. "He was actually laughing to himself when he left the room—only a short while after his colleague Azriel Moshe was murdered. He admitted that he hated Moshe, and claimed that everyone on the team did, too. Gerhard must have found something terribly funny about our conversation, but I'm not sure what it was."

"Think about what he told us," said Hunter. "When I asked him about any secrets he might know, he said he'd tell us one that we would find interesting, but he didn't say he was telling us all of his secrets. He began laughing when he told us that Krista Scelba loved him. That tells us something important..."

"And that is?" said Weems.

"Remember what he said when I asked him about how he felt about her. He said that she wasn't his type. . . which conventionally we would understand to mean not my type of woman. But in this case, where everything is upside down and inside out, we have to consider the possibility—"

"That he's gay, too," interjected Weems. "This case is too much. We have a bizarre kind of sexual comedy going on."

"It's permeated with irony," replied Hunter. "Look what we have, or seem to have. We can't jump to conclusions and it may be that we're being led astray. What we've heard, so far, suggests that Dovet is crazy about Pagetsky, who can't stand him. We can't be sure who she's in love with, but if she's gay, and she's in love with someone on the team, it would have to be Krista Scelba. And Scelba, who is straight, is—if Gerhard is correct—in love with him, but she's not his type. If he's gay, and if he's in love with someone on the team, it would have to have been either Moshe or Dovet."

"Is it possible that Dovet is also gay," Hunter continued, "and that his being infatuated with Pagetsky is just a pose? If so, and he, too, was involved with someone on the team, it would have to be either Moshe or Gerhard. So, it might have been a lover's quarrel that was responsible for Moshe's death. That's always a possibility. Except for one thing—Moshe was, so it seems, straight—described by Gerhard as a sexual predator. We know Moshe slept with Pagetsky in Russia and wanted to continue doing so here in San Francisco."

"We don't know that Moshe slept with Pagetsky. We were told he did. He may have been the only member of the team who wasn't gay—though it may be that none of the members of the team are gay and they're trying to throw us off the trail, one way or another," Hunter added. "Or that all of them are gay."

"This is the weirdest and most confusing case I can remember," said Weems. "There are only five people involved in the case, and four suspects, but who they loved and hated, what their sexual orientation was, and what they were investigating with the Kabbalah is beyond me."

"Maybe professor Scelba will be able to throw some light on the case. There are all kinds of questions she can answer," said Hunter. "Such as, was she having an affair with Moshe? Did he dump her to pursue Pagetsky? Did Scelba know that Pagetsky was in love with her? Is she really in love with Gerhard? And where does Dovet fit in to all of this? Maybe she'll be able to straighten things out for us. Please ask Officer Kook to bring her here. This could be most interesting."

All known religious beliefs, whether simple or complex, present one common characteristic: they presuppose a classification of all things, real and idea, of which men think, into two classes or opposed groups, generally designated by two distinct terms which are translated well enough by the words *profane* and *sacred* (*profane, sacré*). This division of the world into two domains, the one containing all that is sacred, the other all that is profane, is the distinctive trait of religious thought; the beliefs, myths, dogmas and legends are either representations or systems of representations which express the nature of sacred things, the virtues and powers which are attributed to them, or their relations with each other and with profane things. But by sacred things one must not understand simply those personal beings which are called gods or spirits; a rock, a tree, a spring, a pebble, a piece of wood, a house, in a word, anything can be sacred. A rite can have this character; in fact, the rite does not exist which does not have it to a certain degree. There are words, expressions and formulae which can be pronounced only by the mouths of consecrated persons; there are gestures and movements which everybody cannot perform. . . in all the history of human thought there exists no other example of two categories of things so profoundly differentiated or so radically opposed to one another. (1952:52-53)

- Emile Durkheim, *The Elementary Forms of Religious Life*

9

The Painted Lady

THE PAINTED LADY

A few minutes later, Krista Scelba, a woman of about forty, was ushered into the interrogation room. She had short blond hair and blue eyes and was wearing a fashionably designed light blue dress. She had blue eye shadow that matched her dress and painted eyebrows above her natural ones. Her large, dark eyelashes were pasted on and her face was heavily made up with a thick, pearly foundation. Her lips were painted a brilliant blue. In her ears she had large silver earrings and around her neck she wore a pearl necklace. Hunter felt there was something slightly grotesque about her appearance. She walked slowly and hesitantly sat down. Her eyes were red and her face was a drawn. She'd been doing a great deal of crying.

"How can I help you?" she asked in a weak voice.

She suddenly started crying.

Hunter passed her a tissue, which she took with her left hand.

"Thank you," she said, as she wiped the tears from her eyes.

"I can see that the events that took place this morning have been very traumatic for you," Hunter said softly. "It's not unusual for people to become terribly upset in such cases. Relax. All we want to do is find out what happened this morning and learn something about your colleagues."

"Yes, yes... I understand," she said. "The first part of your question is easy for me to answer. Our team generally met in the mornings to discuss our plans and any problems we were facing in getting started with this project. It might seem like a very simple matter to bring together four scholars, with different areas of academic specialization, to investigate something. But if you want to end with something more than four disparate studies, there has to be a certain amount of planning. We also faced problems in terms of what, exactly, each of us was going to do and how our individual efforts would contribute to a true interdisciplinary study of the Kabbalah. The Kabbalah, as you probably recognize by now, is a very complicated matter. It's a movement that stretches back into antiquity and is an arcane body of knowledge that is incredibly difficult to understand. It has a holy book, the *Zohar*, that is also remarkably enigmatic. Kabbalists are not only Jews, but also Catholics, Protestants and Muslims. So what do you focus your attention on? How do you best make sense of the Kabbalah and the Kabbalists, ancient and modern? We had quite a number of things to discuss."

"Yes, I can see that," said Hunter. "I've never quite understood what all this talk about interdisciplinary studies was all about. I've come across it in other cases in which I was involved. But now I'm beginning to get a better picture."

"There is some question about whether the movement for interdisciplinary studies has petered out," she said. "In the final analysis, it hasn't accomplished that much. The best scholars, in whatever their fields, tend to cross disciplines. So does it make sense to have teams of scholars trying to do the same thing? One reason that people are beginning to have their doubts about the interdisciplinary movement in universities is that it hasn't led to any important breakthroughs. Nothing terribly important has come out of all the effort expended. So, although from a logical or theoretical perspective, interdisciplinary teams seem like a good idea, from a practical one, their promise hasn't been realized."

"If that's the case," asked Weems, "why did you become part of this team?"

"I've been asking myself the same thing," she replied. "I thought this team would finally show the value of interdisciplinary approaches to research questions. Also, San Francisco is a lovely city and the idea of spending some time here was very appealing. I'm fascinated by the Kabbalah movement. As a sociologist of religion, the opportunity to participate in a team of scholars investigating the Kabbalah from a number of different scholarly perspectives excited me, even though I recognized the difficulties involved. So I guess all those reasons combined. It's hard to know why people do things. That's one of the questions we were investigating. Why do people become involved with the Kabbalah? How is it, in an age of science, that the study of the Kabbalah has become so fashionable? Why have movie stars and celebrities become students of the Kabbalah? And how is it that this movement has kept itself going for thousands of years?"

"That makes sense to me," said Hunter "I can understand why you joined the team. But I'm not sure what, exactly, you were going to do in your research."

"People ask me that a lot," she replied. She was becoming more animated as the conversation moved into her area of interest. "After all, I'm a sociologist and many people wonder why sociologists might be interested in religion. They imagine that religion should be left to the province of theologians and priests and rabbis, and now we'd add imams and mullahs, I guess."

"That's the way I've always looked at things," said Weems.

"In actuality," replied Scelba, "sociologists have always been interested in religion. One of the classics of sociological analysis, Emile Durkheim's book, *The Elementary Forms of Religious Life*, dealt with a sociological approach to religion. Durkheim argued that religious people divided the world into two opposing realms—the sacred and the profane. The very fact that you have a realm called 'the sacred' implies, Durkheim argued, its opposite, namely 'the profane.' That's because our language makes sense of the world by setting up differences and the most important differences are oppositional ones. A famous linguist, de Saussure, said that in languages there are only differences. Concepts, he argued, are purely differential and are defined not by any positive content they have but negatively, by their relations with other terms. He said that the most precise characteristic of a concept involves it being what others are not. That is, we make sense of the world by seeing it in terms of oppositions—rich and poor, high and low, powerful and weak, and, in this case, sacred and profane. So there has to be a 'profane' if the concept 'sacred' is to mean anything."

"Very interesting," said Hunter.

"Now Durkheim made another important point about religion in his book. He argued that the fundamental categories of all human thought, including science, are religious in origin, and that all our most important social institutions were born of religion. So from this point of view, you can see that religion is of great importance and interest to sociologists. In fact, Durkheim argued that the very idea of society is, in the final analysis, a religious one. Remember, sociology is the study of institutions, of collective behavior, of what people do in groups. So there's good reason for sociologists to study religion, in general, and specific religions or religious sects, in particular. There are many questions for us to consider: religion and socio-economic status, religion and race, religion and gender, religion and ethnicity, religion and politics, religion and sexuality, the functions of religion for different groups of people. The list is endless. I would imagine that given this list of our interests, you can see why a sociologist of religion might find the Kabbalah movement an extremely interesting one to investigate."

"I can understand your interest, as a sociologist, in religion," replied Hunter. "But where does the Kabbalah come in? Why the

Kabbalah and not some other religion or sect, or whatever?"

"That's a reasonable question," Scelba answered. "One thing that is particularly interesting to me, as a sociologist of religion, is how the Kabbalah movement was able to maintain itself and flourish over the centuries, when other movements in Judaism have come and gone. One reason it has been so successful is that it helped its adherents cope with their anxieties about their place in the world. You have to remember that when the Jews were forced to leave Spain in 1492, it was a very traumatic event for them and many Jews were looking for some way to deal with the psychological blows caused by their exile. Christians, on the other hand, argued that the exile of the Jews was some kind of divine punishment for not accepting Christ as the Messiah.

"What the Kabbalah did was supply Jews with a sense of power and righteousness, a sense of their spiritual potency. And a feeling that God was directly and intimately involved in their affairs—what Jews term *Shekhinah*. Like all adherents of mystical religions and sects, the Kabbalists had a strong sense of certitude and power—for they were privy, they believed, to a secret and esoteric knowledge hidden from ordinary people, including Jews who were not Kabbalists. Remember, the *Zohar* exists as a commentary and explication of the Torah, and Kabbalists argue that their arcane knowledge helps them 'unlock' the true meaning of words and phrases and the real significance of the stories found in the Torah."

"So the Kabbalists think that they're right and everyone else is wrong. Is that correct?" asked Weems. "Is this basically a Jewish version of the Christian 'pie in the sky when you die' notion?"

Scelba smiled.

"You do have a blunt way of putting things, Sergeant Weems. But, in a sense, what you've said is correct. In the *Zohar* there's a passage that states that those who argue that the Torah contains only common sayings and ordinary stories are mistaken, for if that were the case, people could compose their own sayings and stories that were even better than those found in the Torah. No, the

Torah only *seems* to be simply written. Remember for Jews—for Orthodox Jews, that is—the Torah contains the words of God. For Kabbalists, the different Hebrew letters, the names of people, and the stories in the Torah all contain hidden meanings and are what might be described as divine mysteries. And it's the *Zohar*, Kabbalists believe, that is the key to unlocking these mysteries.

"One fascinating aspect of the Kabbalah," she added, "was that a number of Christian thinkers tried to subvert the Kabbalah and make it into something Christian in nature. They argued that the Kabbalah was really a kind of Christian revelation and they tried to show that the various elements of Kabbalistic thought could be shown to be, when decoded, connected to Christian beliefs—such as the Trinity, the notion of a Messiah who was the son of God, and that kind of thing. Christian thinkers such as 'Doctor Illuminatus' Raymond Lully and Pico della Mirandola became interested in the Kabbalah and in showing how it really should be seen as a form of Christian revelation. In the seventeenth century, however, when more parts of the *Zohar* and other Kabbalistic writings were translated, and Christian theologians could see what they contained, their fervor cooled and they concluded that they couldn't really turn the *Zohar* into a Christian text.

"We see, then, that Christians have been interested in the Kabbalah for a long time, which may explain why it's popular now with large number of singers, movie stars and others who weren't born Jews. Lots of people nowadays are interested in esoteric knowledge and occult mysteries."

"Speaking of mysteries," interjected Hunter, "I'd like to ask you a few questions about the one we're investigating. It may not be as interesting as the Kabbalah, but it's something terribly important."

"Yes...of course," answered Scelba.

"What can you tell us about the events that took place earlier this morning—from the time your group got together until now?" asked Hunter. "Did anything unusual happen? Did you notice anything different about what went on? How others looked? We're looking for anything, no matter how insignificant it might seem to you, that will help us get to the bottom of this murder."

Scelba sighed as the memory of the traumatic events of the day came flooding back to her mind.

"It was a day like all the others before it," she said. "As you probably know, from talking with those who preceded me, we usually met in the mornings from 9:00 AM until noon, when we broke for lunch. Generally, we had the rest of the day off, though we were going to have an afternoon meeting today for some reason. In our meetings we worked on the research plan for our investigation: who was going to do what, how we were going to integrate our findings. That sort of thing. The idea was that once we worked out our research plan, in future meetings—which were only to be held weekly—we would present our preliminary findings."

"Why were these preliminary findings of interest?" asked Weems.

"Because the information in them might be of use to our colleagues, might give them ideas that would help them in their investigations. This kind of thing can be very helpful. It's similar to the way the human mind works. Sometimes you get ideas from out of the blue and these ideas turn your attention to other ideas you had that you thought weren't important but now, suddenly, become very interesting."

"What was Azriel Moshe like?" asked Hunter. "I take it, from some of the conversations we've had with your colleagues, that he wasn't the easiest person in the world to get along with."

"That's not true," she replied, her face suddenly showing anger. "Azriel was a truly wonderful person—kind, gentle, and very supportive. His only fault was that he was too forgiving of others. His book, *The Mind of the Mystic: An Approach to Kabbalah,* is considered a classic. And he wrote a dozen other important books on the Kabbalah. You have to realize, Azriel had an international reputation. He was a world-class scholar of the very highest caliber. I'm afraid that my colleagues, except for Leon, that is, were jealous of him and resented him. Academic mediocrites love company. Most people have unrealistic notions about themselves and this includes academics. They think they are smarter than they really are, they think they are more important than they really are, they think they write better than they really do, and they want, desperately, to preserve these illusions. They do so by finding other colleagues who they recognize aren't a threat to their sense of esteem. They don't necessarily do this consciously..."

"So you're suggesting that his colleagues were jealous of professor Moshe? Is that what you're saying?" asked Hunter. "I can understand that in a department, but in a randomly organized group of scholars? It doesn't make sense."

"It does if you understand social dynamics," she replied. "In academic institutions professors can find functional alternatives to their desire for power and esteem. They do this by becoming important committee types, academic politicos, administrators. They transfer their need for academic achievement from the world of ideas and scholarship to that of institutional management and become cogs in the machine. There are something like ten thousand sociologists in the United States and only a few hundred of them actually do important research. Most of the people who teach sociology have all kinds of excuses for not doing any research—though it's actually better to have a few hundred very smart people doing research and the others teaching. But even among those who do research, there are many charlatans and confidence men.

"Attitude, you must understand, is everything. If you haven't been productive, and your dean asks you why, you explain that you are thinking outside the box, that you are ahead of your time, that you are pondering immensely complicated and difficult matters, and that your work is theoretically important—so you can't be expected to crank out articles the way various 'hacks' in your department do. But when you do publish the results of your research, you assert, confidently, you will stand your discipline on its head and you, and the dean who stood by you, will bask in glory. If you have published something and it has not been well received, you explain that you are ahead of your time and that it will only be a matter of time before the importance of your contributions are recognized. It also helps if you can write in a somewhat unintelligible manner, like certain French intellectuals who are popular in the United States. It's the air of confidence that you project to others—even if your knees are shaking like crazy when you talk to them about your work—in which you suggest, without the slightest sense that you could be wrong, that you are a star—that is all important."

"You're making professors sound more and more like con men," said Hunter. "Surely, you're exaggerating."

"Perhaps, a bit. But not that much," replied Krista Scelba. "Half are confidence men and the other half are fools. The members of our team, let me point out, lest you get the wrong idea, are all scholars of the first rank, who don't have to play those kinds of games. But the politics were no different. In this research team that Azriel assembled, everyone thought of himself or herself as a super-star, so the jealousy everyone felt was even more intense. The members of the team are quite distinguished, but they all paled next to Azriel. Kind of sad, if you think about it."

"I take it, from what you've told us, that the person who felt the most hostility towards Azriel would be Leon Gerhard, who claimed that Azriel stole his ideas. Is that correct?"

"There is some question in my mind," she replied, "as to whether Leon is telling the truth about this matter. I would surmise that he inflated the importance of any ideas he might have shared with Azriel. Azriel had more than enough ideas to last a lifetime. He didn't need to steal them from Leon. Leon, I might add, is a brilliant scholar; he just wasn't in the same league as Azriel. I'm very fond of Leon, really I am. But you should know he has a tendency to exaggerate things. For example, he has this crazy idea that I'm in love with him. It's an absurd notion. But he is witty and very charming."

"I sense a kind of ambivalence in your feelings about Gerhard," said Hunter.

"I like him a lot, but I can see his shortcomings. Yes, that's a good way of putting it," she replied. "Nobody's perfect, and seeing flaws in people we like is an important step in having a decent relationship with them. Azriel had his flaws, too. We all have our flaws."

"We've heard different things about his relationship with Svelana Pagetsky," said Hunter. "We've even heard that Azriel and you were having, shall we say, an intimate relationship, and that suddenly, for no reason that anyone has told us about, he dropped you and turned his attentions in her direction."

Krista Scelba's face suddenly became flushed and she started breathing heavily.

"It's true that we had a very strong emotional bond between us. I was intoxicated by Azriel's mind. It was so fertile, so creative. Just spending time with him was exciting, as ideas came cascading out of his head. But if our relationship deteriorated, it most certainly wasn't because he left me and turned his attentions, as you so delicately put it, towards Svetlana. We had what I thought would be a temporary falling out over something unimportant. You know it's often trivial things that lead to spats and these spats lead to arguments, and before you know it, a relationship is damaged. Not irreparably in our case—or so I believed."

"What about Jean-Pascal Dovet? How does he fit into the picture?" asked Hunter. "It's curious, but nobody that we've interviewed had very much to say about him."

"Jean-Pascal is first and foremost a physician. He is always acting as what he is, a neurologist. They tend, as a rule, to be smug, feeling that their specialty and their realm of knowledge is something exceptional. Very much like the Kabbalists, actually. Also, he's French, and French intellectuals and scholars are all, to my way of thinking, a bit strange. Their writing is unintelligible to most people, though large numbers of academics, especially Americans, seem to think they understand what they've written. Again, now that I think about it, it's like the Kabbalists. We have writings that seem unintelligible but which some adherents think are of remarkable importance. One connection we can make, interestingly enough, is that many of these inscrutable French writers are Jewish.

"In any case, Jean-Pascal's book *NeuroKabbalah* is, to my way of thinking, both unintelligible and, for those parts I could understand, full of nonsense. His thesis was that, if I interpret him correctly, the Kabbalah was a perfect representation or simulacrum of the human brain. Quite audacious, if you think about it. I liked that quality about Jean-Pascal. His mind always seemed to be three steps ahead of you when you got into a discussion of any topic. So he was always making suggestions that, when you first heard them, seemed quite far-fetched. But then, when you thought about them, seemed as if they might be interesting to pursue."

"Speaking of pursuits," Hunter said, "is it true that he was bedazzled by Svetlana Pagetsky? We've had hints, from various people that this was the case, though she told us she felt he was very cold towards her."

"When you introduce an attractive women into a situation, all kinds of remarkable things are possible. When our team had its first meeting, a number of weeks ago, there were three men and two women. Svetlana, you must realize, presents herself as a combination intellectual and beauty queen—you get that notion from the way she dresses, from the way she carries herself, from the way she speaks. Personally speaking, I think she's an attractive woman but not really beautiful. To tell the truth, I think she looks cheap and her taste is vulgar. Her clothes aren't the kind you get at the best shops, not by any means. But she seemed to be so utterly convinced of her beauty that I think she carried the men along with her in that respect.

"It's strange, but many Russian women are quite slender and quite attractive when they are young, but when they turn forty, they get fat. I'm not exactly sure why. It must have something to do with the national character. In any case, Svetlana's performance— her projection of herself as a radiant beauty—seemed to captivate all the men on the team. I'm not sure whether she was always successful or how long it lasted; Jean-Pascal seemed taken with her for a while, and so were Azriel and Leon. I can't be sure whether they were actually hypnotized by her or were merely playing along with her. You never can tell about these things. So while our meetings were very business-like and focused on our research program, there was always this hidden undercurrent involving possible sexual relations between Svetlana and other members of the team. The male members of the team might have enjoyed it, but I found it terribly disconcerting, at the very least. But whether she was actually involved with anyone on the team is hard to say. I don't have any information on this matter. She could have been sleeping with any of the members of the team—or with all of them, at the same time—but I can't say."

"I see," said Hunter. "Tell us, what did you do after the meeting broke up?"

"I went to my office. A group of us were supposed to go to lunch. I called Jean-Pascal to find out about something and then was interrupted by someone who came by and had a brief chat while Jean-Pascal waited on the phone. Then we resumed our conversation. Shortly after that I heard Felliyanka screaming and rushed into Azriel's office and saw him there, lying on the floor with that dagger in his back."

"I see," said Hunter. "You've been very helpful and I want to thank you for your assistance. We've learned a good deal—both about why sociologists might be interested in the Kabbalah and about professor Moshe's team. Sergeant Weems will escort you back to the room where your colleagues are gathered. I'm going to let you all go home now. We'll gather together in the seminar room tomorrow morning at 10:00 AM."

"Talcott," he said. "Will you please escort professor Scelba back to the room where her colleagues are waiting? Tell them they can go home, and that we'll meet here tomorrow at 10:00 AM, in the seminar room. Remind them that they'll all be under police protection."

"Will do," said Weems.

After Weems and Scelba left the room where the interrogation had taken place, Hunter took another look at Azriel Moshe's journal. There was a discussion of heaven and hell that interested him.

I attended a dinner party at a friend's house the other day. There were seven of us—three couples and myself, the "odd man" out, as usual. It turns out that each of the couples had brought a cake and the hostess had made a few cakes on her own, so there were six different kinds of cakes and cookies served for dessert... almost one for each person.

"Just think of all the empty calories on this table. It's sheer hell for anyone trying to look after his weight," I said.

"No," said the hostess, who was very slim, "it's sheer heaven."

"I'm convinced that the devil created pastry chefs," I said. "And heaven is where you can go to a party and when there are six cakes on the table, you can eat as much as you want of each of the cakes and not gain any weight."

"If that's heaven, what's hell like?" asked the host.

"Hell is where you go to a dinner party and there are six cakes served for dessert. You can't eat any of them but you gain the weight you would have put on if you had eaten all of them."

"It's a case of 'no pie in the sky when you die'," he said.

"Yes, in a sense. And that makes me wonder. If here, on earth, we have six cakes for dessert, when we die and go to heaven does that mean we'll have twelve cakes? And if we die and go to hell, does that mean we'll only have three cakes, but no pies?"

I restrained myself and had very small slices of each of the cakes, since I wanted to see what they were like. But I wonder whether it would have been better, in the sense of having more pleasure, for me to have larger slices of only three of the cakes?

So—you can take the bocher out of the Yeshiva, but you can't stop his mind from working the way Talmudic scholars have worked over the centuries. Maybe I've been reading too many of those Kabbalistic documents and too many commentaries by Torah schol-

ars. You have to admire the way they analyzed things. Every word had significance and they performed prodigious feats of analysis.

"I wonder what a 'bocher' is?" thought Hunter as he read the manuscript. "I know what Yeshivas are. The word is vaguely similar to 'book' so it might have something to do with book reading and study?"

His thoughts were interrupted by Weems, who had come back from returning Krista Scelba to the room where the other suspects were waiting.

"I told them to come back at 10:00 AM tomorrow and that we'd be providing police protection for them tonight. They didn't like the idea, but I explained that they were in danger and should stay home tonight," he said.

Weems noticed that Hunter had been reading Moshe's journal.

"Can't keep away from Moshe's journal, can you?" he added.

"You can't imagine how interesting it is," Hunter replied. "It reveals a lot about Moshe's mind, and his interests. And he had insights that he drew from everything you can think of. That seems typical of certain kinds of Jewish scholars who are involved in studying Torah, or who are into the Kabbalah."

"What did you make of Professor Scelba?" asked Weems. "To me, with all that makeup, she looks like a cheap hooker."

Hunter laughed.

"I think you're being too harsh, Talcott," replied Hunter. "It may be that Italian women use lots of makeup. And some men probably like that painted look. The question in my mind is whether that look appealed to Jean-Pascal Dovet or Leon Gerhard. And how long it appealed to Azriel Moshe."

The *Zohar* is the first book in which the theory of the four methods of interpreting Scripture, originally developed by Christian exegetes, is taken up by a Jewish author. But of the four layers of meaning: the literal, the Aggadic or homiletic, the allegorical, and the mystical, in the last resort only the fourth—*Raza,* i.e. "The Mystery," in the terminology of the *Zohar*—matters to the author. It's true that he also advances numerous examples of Scriptural interpretation based on the other three methods, but these are either taken from other writings or, at the most, developed from ideas not peculiar to Kabbalism... And, as we have seen, the "mystery" in every case concerns the interpretation of the Biblical word as a symbol pointing to the hidden word of God and its inner processes. (1946:210)

- Gershom Sholem, *Major Trends in Jewish Mysticism*

10

An Interview with Fatima Vescica

Leon Gerhard had loaded the last of his dinner plates into the dishwasher in his cramped one bedroom apartment, and shut it with a click. He picked up the paper off the kitchen table and moved into the den, searching among his pockets for a pair of glasses. Finding them, he settled back and began reading *The New York Times*. After a few minutes he decided to rest his eyes for a few minutes, only to be awoken by a phone call.

"Is this Rabbi Gerhard?" a woman asked.

"Yes...yes, it is," he replied.

"Allow me to introduce myself. My name is Fatima Vescica."

"The rock singer?" he asked.

"Yes," she replied. "I got your name from our mutual friend, Rabbi Hiyyah, in Los Angeles. I hope I'm not interrupting your dinner?"

"No, not at all," he replied.

"I'm in town for a gig at the Oakland Coliseum tomorrow night, and I've got a bit of free time tonight. Is it possible to see you? Rabbi Hiyyah said you're one of the world's leading authorities on the Kabbalah and I've got some questions I'd like answered. I was hoping you could spare a few minutes to see me. We can meet wherever it would be convenient for you; I can send my limo to pick you up."

"We can meet in my apartment," he said. "There was a tragedy at the University today. A member of a team of Kabbalah scholars I belong to was murdered. So I can't leave my apartment. But if you want to come here, I can spare you a bit of time."

"Cool," said the singer. "I'll be there in fifteen minutes or so."

"I... I look forward to meeting you," Gerhard said, and hung up.

"This is quite strange," he thought. "It's been quite a remarkable day. And now I'm to have a chat with Fatima. I read in the paper that she was interested in the Kabbalah. But why? Is she going to have rabbis in black hats and long black coats in her next music video? I've never met a pop celebrity. I wonder what she'll be like." He got up, and spent some time making sure his apartment was nice and tidy, and then thought about whether he should change his brown sweater or not. Should he have a copy of the *Zohar* with him, or would this be more of a chat?

Soon there was a light knock on the door.

He got up and opened the door. Standing in front of him was a short, slender woman of about forty, with dyed blonde hair, in a long black coat with a hood. Her coat was open and she was wearing, underneath it, a tight fitting tee shirt and a mini skirt the color of a *caffé latte*. Her stockings and shoes were the same color. He couldn't decide whether she was pretty or not. He'd seen some of her videos and in them she exuded glamour and sexiness, but up close, in the flesh, she seemed no different from any other forty-year-old woman.

"Fatima, won't you come in?" he asked. "It's a pleasure to meet you."

She walked in, unzipped her coat, and sat down on his sofa. "It's good of you to see me," she said. "I've become very interested in the Kabbalah. Or is it in Kabbalah? And not because studying Kabbalah is trendy and the thing to do in Los Angeles, which it is, even for Catholics like myself. In any case, there's something about the stories in the *Zohar* that strike a chord with me. And the ten emanations of Ein Sof have a mystical quality that I find very compelling. But I can't explain why that diagram, with its ten circles, has this effect. You're a rabbi and an expert on Kabbalah. Maybe you can clue me in to what's going on in that diagram? What is it, in particular, about Kabbalah that's so fascinating? Why does it give such good vibes?"

Gerhard smiled.

"You're not the first person to have this reaction," he replied. "You have to realize that we live in what is essentially a rational age, at least in the western world. Science is dominant and scientific experimentation and proofs of assertions by empirical evidence are the common mode of making acceptable statements about the world. Kabbalah is just the opposite. It offers a mystical and magical approach to the world that focuses on God's words to us and on the Torah, which Kabbalists believe represents God's many faces. It also deals with what they claim is secret and mystical knowledge that is hidden in the *Zohar*, which is, you must realize, an attempt to fathom the secrets in the Torah. So Kabbalah feeds upon the fact that large number of people do not find scientific rationalism satisfactory. The society in which science dominates is, to many people, hollow and uninteresting. It doesn't satisfy our need to know our place in the universe and our sense that there is some kind of a power—we call it God or Ein Sof—that we feel exists and that we want to know more about."

"Yes, I can follow that," she said. "You're talking about people in general. But why should Kabbalah be of interest to me? I'm a Roman Catholic and we've got saints and all kinds of religious mumbo-jumbo in our religion. Enough to satisfy anyone, I would imagine."

"I know. I've seen all the religious imagery you use in your videos, such as your music-video for the song 'Like a Prayer'," said Gerhard.

"You've seen my videos?" she replied, in astonishment.

"Rabbis are human beings like anyone else," he answered. "And Jews, you must remember, are not ascetic. It's not part of our religion. We value sexual relations, we value pleasure, we value the good things in life, and we believe that by doing so, in the proper way, we're bringing ourselves closer to God. In Judaism there are many feasts and communal celebrations. Jews celebrate together. Before we go any further, I just need to ask something for my own comfort. Are you planning on using images of Orthodox Jews and Jewish mystics in your next music video? Are we going to replace the virgins, priests, nuns and churches with menorahs, symbols from the kabbalah, rabbis, and synagogues?"

She broke out laughing.

"No, that's not why I'm interested in Kabbalah," she said. "What a funny video that would be; large numbers of orthodox Jews, at some meeting they have. They're all sitting, row after row of men in black suits and hats, with white shirts and dark ties, in huge rooms on both sides of long tables. I can see myself in a brilliant red sequined pantsuit, that vaguely revealed my breasts, suddenly appearing and dancing in front of them on a table, gyrating and shimmying wildly, as they sit, hypnotized. Then the video would cut away to a wedding, where men and women are dancing to Kletzmer music, and waiters are running back and forth with trays laden with Jewish food—kugel and herring and stuff like that. A group of bearded men are dancing around someone. Suddenly they all converge on this person and raise her up. It's me, standing on a chair, in a diaphanous white gown. They set me down and I tear off my gown, revealing a thin see-through white shirt and a micro mini skirt. I do a wild dance to the lyrics of some song I've written for the occasion. Eventually another woman joins in, then a man, then everyone in line dances. Next we cut to an image of me in some town in Israel in front of an old synagogue or some other holy place. Maybe at the Wailing Wall. It's deserted and I'm the only one there, in a long black coat, with a hood, like the one I'm wearing. The moon is full and in the moonlight I do a dance as the song I'm singing changes into a minor key... How does that sound? Your deepest fears realized?"

Then she laughed.

"I hadn't thought very much about using Jewish imagery, but now that you mention it, I think it might work. I wonder how I could work in the Kabbalah..." she said. "That's another thing I wanted to ask you. The Kabbalah is terribly abstract. I can't understand it in terms of concrete images. Maybe that's part of the appeal? It's a kind of powerful presence that I feel but I can't put my finger on. The Ein Sof and the ten Sefirot form some kind of an abstract system in which everything in the universe is linked to everything else, mysteries piled upon mysteries in the *Zohar*, which Kabbalah study promises to reveal. I think the idea that by studying Kabbalah you know lots of things that other people don't know, that you can see important meanings in things that seem, to others, trivial and of no consequence — that's what I like about it."

She paused.

"Hmm... maybe I've answered my own question," she said. "Maybe its because I'm a Catholic and believe that there is some kind of a holy presence working in the world that I dig Kabbalah, except that I think Kabbalah is the key to finding out the mysteries that interest me, and not Catholic theology, which is terribly repressive, from my point of view. Maybe that's it?"

"That's quite possible," replied Gerhard.

Suddenly, Fatima's coat started beeping.

"Damn," she said. "If you don't mind, I'd like to answer my phone.

Gerhard nodded.

She grabbed her coat and after fumbling around for a while, found her cell phone.

"Yes," she said. "What's up?"

She listened for a few moments.

"Shit!" she said."I'll come right away."

"You must forgive me," she said. "But there's trouble with the lighting system for my show and I've got to get to the Coliseum and talk with the lighting people there."

"Can I call a cab for you?" asked Gerhard.

"No, I've got a limo waiting for me in front of your building."

She quickly put on her coat.

"I can't thank you enough," she said. "You've been very helpful. More than you can imagine. I'll have my PR people send you some signed posters as a sign of my appreciation."

She walked over and shook hands with Gerhard.

"Shalom," she said.

Then she opened the door to his apartment and left. Gerhard watched her sweep out into the hall, and looked out the window of his apartment. A long black limousine was parked right in front of his apartment behind a police car. Fatima emerged from his building, and the driver opened the door to her limo. As she got in the limousine she looked up and saw Gerhard watching her from his window. She blew him a kiss, got into her card, and the driver closed the door of the limousine, which sped off into the night.

Shekhina is the frequently used Talmudic term denoting the visible and audible manifestations of God's presence on earth. In its ultimate development as it appears in the late Midrash literature, the Shekhina concept stood for an independent, feminine divine entity prompted by her compassionate nature to argue with God in defense of man. She is thus, if not by character, then by function and position, a direct heir to such ancient Hebrew goddesses of Canaanite origin as Asherah and Anath. (1990:37)

- Raphael Patai, *The Hebrew Goddess*

11

Krista Scelba Writes a Letter

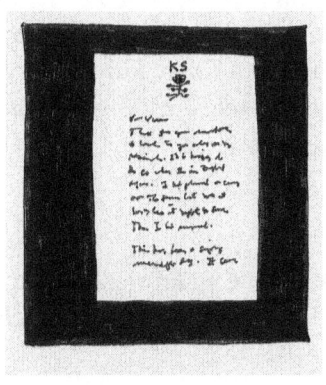

When she arrived back at her apartment on Jones Street, the first thing Krista Scelba did was pour herself a Campari on ice. She liked the way the bitter flavor of the Campari jarred her taste buds, and she liked its rich, red color.

She had a bit of dinner and then decided to write a letter to her best friend, Victoria Gainsborough, a fellow professor of history at Sussex University in England.

Dear Victoria:

Thanks for your invitation to lecture to your class on my research. I'll be happy to do so when I'm in England again. I had planned on coming over the summer but now it looks like it might be sooner than I had imagined.

This has been a simply incredible day. It seems that Azriel Moshe, the leader of our research team, was murdered. And I'm afraid the police think I did it. The inspector who questioned me didn't say that, of course, but I got that message from the tone of his voice and his body language. The inspector, one Solomon Hunter, is something of a dandy and not too bright. At least I got that impression when he interrogated me and asked the most incredible questions—about my love life, my research and all kinds of other personal things. He has a moronic assistant, also— a dyspeptic person who seems to have an aversion to academics of all or any kind.

In any case, it looks like my research into the sociological aspects of the Kabbalah will not continue. I'll have to put it off until this horrid murder is cleared up and I've had some time to recuperate from all the stress it generated. I'm thinking of a couple of months at the beach. Maybe in Thailand or some other exotic area, as far away from the Kabbalah and San Francisco as I can get. When the murderer has been found and the case has been resolved, I'll have to think about the next step. Today has been too traumatic for me. I need to get away and relax, to forget about poor Azriel Moshe and this whole disastrous adventure.

Love,
Krista

After she wrote the letter, she took a shower and went to bed.

"What a terrible day this has been," she thought, before she fell into a deep sleep.

Man becomes aware of the sacred because it manifests itself, shows itself, as something wholly different from the profane. To designate the *act of manifestation* of the sacred, we have proposed the term *hierophany*. It's a fitting term, because it does not imply anything further; it expresses no more than is implicit in its etymological content, i.e., that *something sacred shows itself to us*. It could be said that the history of religions—from the most primitive to the most highly developed—is constituted by a great number of hierophanies, by manifestations of sacred realities. From the most elementary hierophany—e.g., manifestation of the sacred in some ordinary object, a stone or a tree—to the supreme hierophany (which, for a Christian, is the incarnation of God in Jesus Christ) there is no solution of continuity. In each case we are confronted by the same mysterious act—the manifestation of something of a wholly different order, a reality that does not belong to our world, in objects that are an integral part of our natural "profane" world. (1961:11)

- Mircea Eliade, *The Sacred and The Profane: The Nature of Religion*

12

Jean-Pascal Dovet's Phone Call

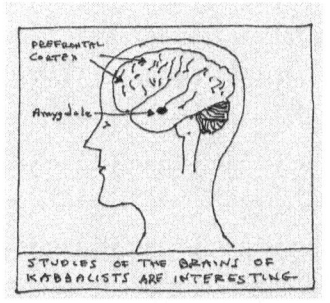

Jean-Pascal Dovet was listing to a Debussy piano trio and sipping a glass of red wine when the phone rang. He hit the pause button on his CD player and the music stopped playing.

"Hello," he said.

"Jean-Pascal....it's Albert Assa," said the voice. "I'm calling from Paris."

"Albert! And how is life at the CNRS? Anything exciting to report?" said Jean-Pascal.

"I'm calling about the article you said you were thinking of writing for our magazine, *Mentalité*. Have you written it yet, by chance?" asked Albert.

"No, I've been remiss, I must confess. I've been thinking about that article a good deal," said Jean-Pascal. "And I was about to begin writing it today, when something remarkable happened. Azriel

Moshe, the director of our Kabbalah research project, was murdered this afternoon. I'm still in a state of shock."

"Murdered?" said Albert. "That's astounding. Simply incredible."

"Yes," said Jean-Pascal, "and what makes things even more remarkable is I believe that the police inspector working on the job thinks I am the killer."

"You? That's simply beyond belief," replied Albert. His voice showed his excitement. "Why do you say that?"

"It's nothing he said," replied Jean-Pascal. "It's just that his body language and his facial expressions indicated that he has an idea lodged in his head—which is that I was the most logical person to kill Azriel Moshe. You know how you get feelings from conversations you have about what people you are talking to think about you? It's nothing you can put your finger on, and I may be mistaken."

"I certainly hope so," said Albert.

"Maybe, if I got to work on that article I promised you, it would take my mind off this madness," said Jean-Pascal. "I think I'll start it tonight. I might as well work since I don't think I can sleep. I was listening to some chamber music and having a glass of wine. Some of this California wine is pretty good, you know."

"What will your thesis be?" asked Albert.

"The article, as my e-mail to you suggested, deals with Kabbalists—the people who study the Kabbalah. It's very popular here in the United States, where there's a large new-age movement and all kinds of religions, some of which seem quite bizarre, are flourishing. Of course Kabbalah is not bizarre, by any means. Jews have been studying Kabbalah for thousands of years and it's an important part of the religion, as you well know. I'm involved— I was involved with a multi-disciplinary team studying the relation between Kabbalah study and various things: mental health, history, sociological aspects, you name it. And, on my front, neurological aspects, and, in particular, trying to find a neurological profile of kabbalists."

"I've looked at EKG's of the brains of kabbalists and done some preliminary magnetic resonance imaging and it looks like there is an unusual amount of electrical activity in certain regions of the brain," he added. "Both when Kabbalists are studying Kabbalah and in periods when they are doing other things. What seems to have happened is that studying the Kabbalah, unlike other forms of mental activity in people, leads to certain nerve channels or pathways being strengthened in remarkable ways. I think this is caused by the fantastic images and the incredible symbology they have created, so that Kabbalah study ultimately becomes very similar, in nature, to an addiction. Kabbalah study seems to charge—electronically, that is—certain areas of the brain which are sources of pleasure. Endorphins are released and a feeling of well-being and plenitude is generated. Quite remarkable. I hoped to get into Positron Emission Tomography, Magnetic Resonance Imaging, Functional Magnetic Resonance Imaging and Computed Tomography with a number of Kabbalists and a control group—maybe Unitarians? But now all of that is off."

"An addiction?" asked Albert. "Like a drug addiction? Is that what you're saying?"

"In many respects, yes," he replied. "Kabbalah study provides intellectual gratifications to its adherents. They believe they are in touch with hidden truths and esoteric knowledge, which some personality types finds attractive. And they think that just about everything hides a secret. For Kabbalists, the world is full of mystery, and things that seem common and ordinary are, in actuality, signifiers of secret knowledge that only those who are part of a select group of people are aware of. What emerges is the neurological channeling that we find in addiction, as certain neurological pathways become dominant and are supported by continued 'doses,' so to speak, of that which has generated the addiction. Kabbalists feel a strong sense of relaxation, of inner pleasure and of well being. I've noted a constriction in their pupils, a slowed pulse, and decreased blood pressure in Kabbalists. All these are phenomena typically associated with drug dependency. Also, like other kinds of addictions, you find the same kind of collective be-havior in Kabbalah that you find in drug culture. Kabbalah study is a group activity, like most everything in Judaism. And being a member of a group that has separated from the ordinary members of the religion, with claims to secret knowledge, confers both a sense of distinctiveness and of identity, which reinforces the habit-forming aspects of Kabbalah study."

"Fascinating," said Albert. "I've never seen anything casting the study of the Kabbalah in in a drug-depency context. Your arti-cle will create a sensation. I just hope you have good evidence to support your position."

"Yes, I know," said Jean-Pascal. "You can look at the EKGs and other data I send and see what you think about it. I had only started gathering data, you know."

"Very fine," said Albert. "Send your article off when it's done. The sooner the better. And good luck with the police."

"I hope I don't need it," said Jean-Pascal. "I hope the inspector is more clever than I think he is. He did know who Maigret is, so maybe there's more to him that I imagine."

With that he hung up the telephone and had a sip of wine. Then he pressed the play button on his CD player and the music came flooding into his apartment.

"When you listen to Debussy," he thought, "isn't it curious how the world seems to be a much more pleasant place than it really is?"

The tree came to express everything that religious man regards as *pre-eminently real and sacred,* everything that he knows the gods to possess of their own nature and that is only rarely accessible to privileged individuals, the heroes and demigods. That is why myths of the quest for youth or immortality give prominent place to a tree with golden fruit or miraculous leaves, a tree growing "in the distant land" (really in the other world) and guarded by monsters (griffins, dragons, snakes). He who would gather its fruits must confront and slay the guardian monster. This in itself tells us that we here have *an initiatory ordeal of the heroic type;* it's by violence that the victor obtains the superhuman, almost divine condition, of eternal youth, invincibility, and unlimited power. (1961:149-150)

- Mircea Eliade, *The Sacred and the Profane*

13

Svetlana and the Patriarchs

When she got to her apartment, the first thing Svetlana did was take a hot bath.

"Hot water. It has a miraculous power," she thought, as she lowered herself into the bath. "A hot bath is just what is needed when things seem to be falling apart."

She luxuriated in the bath for a half hour, relaxing and cleaning herself. She realized she hadn't eaten anything since breakfast and was very hungry. So she got out of the bath and toweled herself dry. Then she got into her nightgown and a bathrobe and walked, in a leisurely manner, to the kitchen. There were some piroshki and blintzes that she had picked up several days before at a Russian delicatessen on Geary street, so she put them on a glass plate and heated them in her microwave for a few minutes. She made a salad of beets, cucumbers and tomatoes and poured some olive oil and a touch of Balsamic vinegar on it. In the cupboard she found some dark Russian pumpernickel bread. It was heavy and had a flaky crust.

"Thank God," she thought, "there are Russians in this city. You can get all kinds of wonderful things in their delicatessens and bakeries. Not that there aren't good Italian and Jewish places here, too. And good bread, even in some supermarkets. Maybe even better than some of the French bread. Their bakers seem to be in decline and some French bread nowadays is like cotton fluff."

She poured herself a shot of Absolut Vodka.

"Here's to myself," she thought, as she lifted her glass and then downed the Vodka in one swallow. "And to the memory of poor Azriel. He would have loved this meal. He was passionate about food."

She recalled that every meal for Azriel was a crisis. God forbid he ordered the wrong dish at a Chinese restaurant, or that some-one cooked his steak too long so it wasn't bloody red. He would brood endlessly about his ordering mistakes, his lost opportunities in restaurants, and about bad meals. And when he ate he tended to say little. He just gazed at the food he was eating and ate it, rapturously, often making comments about how a good meal is a blessing.

"If I had my life to live over," he would say, "I'd live over a good Chinese restaurant. And, if the Gods were really smiling on me, it would be next to a real Jewish delicatessen with the kind of fatty corned beef that would head, immediately after you ate it, directly to your arteries and lodge there until you got some cardiologists to scrape it away."

"No need for cardiologists now," she thought. "Azriel is dead. Murdered, no less. And that damned detective thinks I killed Azriel. That Inspector Hunter...he didn't say anything directly, but I could tell from the way he looked at me, the questions he asked me, and the tone of his voice, that he thinks I'm the killer. Unbelievable. I didn't study semiotics for nothing. I'm sure Hunter thinks I did it. Damn!"

Svetlana then ate, ravenously and then, when she had finished, she realized she hadn't had dessert. So she went to her refrigerator and found some Russian poppy seed cake.

"This, I must have with tea," she thought to herself. "That's the proper thing to have with poppy seed cake."

She made herself a pot of tea, which she had with the cake.

"That was good," she thought, as she finished the piece of poppy seed cake. "A good piece of cake and tea. You can't beat it."

She looked at her watch.

"Damn. It's getting late," she thought. "And I've got to get to the university by 10:00 AM tomorrow for more interrogations. What a mess. The inspector's having Interpol investigate us, too. Who knows what Hunter will find out from them?"

She washed her dishes and put them in her dishwasher. Then she brushed her teeth, looking at them in the mirror and admiring how white and regular they were. She flossed them, carefully, and went to bed. As soon as her head hit her pillow, she was asleep. And then, to her amazement, she found herself in a small, book-lined room, where an old man was writing furiously on a piece of parchment. It was obvious he couldn't see her, that she was invisible. She walked around to the front of the table where he was writing. It was piled high with pieces of paper, each numbered. His eyes were glazed, as if he were in some kind of trance. He seemed to be listening to someone who was telling him what to write—but there was nobody, except for Svetlana, in the room. He wrote at a furious pace, not stopping for anything, except to dip his pen into ink.

Finally, after writing for more than an hour, he closed his eyes, and collapsed onto his desk. He lay, with his head on his arms, for not more than a few minutes, when he suddenly wakened.

"Shroolik!" he yelled. "Tea, Shroolik, tea."

In a few moments, a very tall man, he must have been seven feet tall, came running into the room. He held a tray on which there was a pot of tea, a glass, and some small honey cakes.

"One moment, Reb De Leon," he said. "One moment. I'm not as young or quick as I used to be. And how is the work coming?"

Then she noticed that this tall man was very old. He had red blotches on his face and his hair was white. His wrists were very thin and his fingers were long and bony.

"The book. Ah, the book," said the man who had been writing. "It's progressing. At times it seems that I'm not writing it but that the book is writing me."

He started drinking the tea and eating the small cakes. When he had finished, he said "Now, back to work. Bring me the faces!"

"The faces... yes," said Shroolik. "Once more the faces. Always the faces."

He went to a large bookcase and after looking around for a few moments, took down a huge book. It must have been two feet long. He brought it over to De Leon, who opened it up, thumbed through some pages, and finally, when he found the page he was looking for, opened up the book. In front of him was a fantastic diagram, composed of two circles full of small areas and smaller circles of Hebrew that formed an intricate design. On the top, the circle had rows of small areas underneath it, that looked like an open fan and long lines that attached to the circle below, which was full of small, circular areas that were full of tiny Hebrew characters. At the bottom of the diagram were two lines of Hebrew, that read:

The Holy Beard goes as far as the navel of the Great Face and covers the faces of the Father and the Mother and rests upon the head of the Small Face and the Female.

"The small face," De Leon said, putting his finger on a portion of the diagram and studying it carefully. "The secrets of The Small Face and of The Great Face as well. They still elude me, Shroolik, but I can sense the power emanating from these faces, the power that extends from The Small Face, the angry one, the Godhead, down the thirteen strands of its beard, to The Great Face. The thirteen strands of the beard—they represent, I believe, divine mercy.

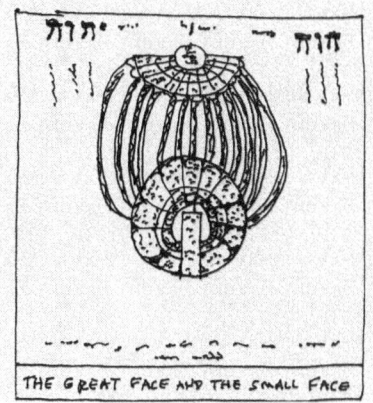

The Great Face and the Small Face

And there are thirteen segments on the small face and thirteen circles of knowledge in the big face. This image—it contains, in it in some marvelous way, Shroolik, all the world and all its mysteries. A divine image, an image that is at the center of the universe. And the Yud Heh Vov Hey, the Tetragrammaton, found in the upper left hand corner. It contains, in some magical way, the 96 names of God and all his 600 faces. The Small Face is, so we are told, the son of the Tetragrammaton and, in addition, the Bridegroom of Shekhinah."

After he said this, he started chanting, rocking his body back and forth and raising his right hand and pointing up, and sometimes pointing down, with one or two fingers, at certain points in his prayers. After a while he stopped. He continued to pray silently to himself.

"Shroolik," he said, "The Sefirot. Bring me the diagram of the ten Sefirot! I need to gaze upon them."

Shroolik rushed to the book case and took out a book, which he brought to De Leon.

"Come. Sit next to me," said De Leon. "Maybe you'll finally learn something. Maybe something will be able to penetrate that thick skull of yours."

Shroolik sat down next to De Leon, at the table where he had several books spread out before him. De Leon turned some pages and came upon the diagram he was looking for—the one of the ten Sefirot.

He spoke to Shroolik.

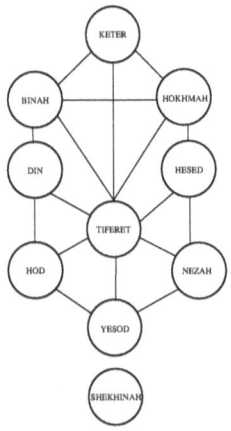

The 10 Sefirot

"There is nothing, Shroolik...nothing," he said, "not even the tiniest thing that you can think of that is not fastened to the links of these Sefirot. Everything is contained in its mystery, its oneness captures everything. God is one and his secret is one, as well. The same applies to all the worlds below and all the worlds above. They also are all one. We cannot divide divine existence into parts. The entire chain in which everything is related to everything else — it, too, is one, down to its very last link. Everything is connected, it has been revealed, with everything else; so divine essence is below as well as above, in heaven and on earth. It includes everything and there is nothing else."

"These ten Sefirot are the secret of existence, Shroolik. They are the array of wisdom by which the worlds both above and below were created. And corresponding to this magnificent secret are the ten holy utterances by which the entire world was created by God and also the ten commandments, which epitomize the holy Torah. Indeed, the ten Sefirot reveal to us all the secrets of divine existence; they comprise both that which is above and that which is below. That is, they comprise everything. They are ancient and they are concealed from most people. From them emerges the mystery of the supernal chariot—a matter concealed and revealed only to those who study the divine writings and discover knowledge. From one bit of existence, from something as insignificant as a stone in a field, the soul can perceive the existence of the entire world and of God, which has neither beginning nor end."

Shroolik nodded.

Then Moses De Leon took a long ram's horn which was lying on his desk. He put the horn to his mouth and blew a long note on it, a note that lingered in the air, that bounced off the walls of the small room in which the two men were sitting.

Svetlana woke with a start.

"Where am I?" she shrieked. "Where did that noise come from?"

Then she realized the sound she heard was from someone's automobile horn and remembered that she was in San Francisco. The sun was just beginning to rise.

Since this study has drawn so heavily upon the work of Max Weber, it's only fitting in this concluding chapter that we examine the relevance of our findings for Weber's theory. As is evident, we have not attempted to test his *historical hypothesis* concerning the relationship between Protestantism and the emergence of the spirit of modern capitalism. We have sought to extract from his many writings on religion the *basic underlying assumption,* and then test it in an analysis of the contemporary scene in one of the major metropolitan communities of the United States. This is the assumption that each of the major religions of the world develops its own distinctive orientation toward all the major phases of human activity, and thus comes to exercise an influence on the development of other major institutional systems in society, an influence which cannot be accounted for in merely economic terms... Our study has provided support for Weber's basic assumption—at least as far as it applies to the major religious groups in contemporary American society. (1963: 356-357)

- Gerhard Lenski, *The Religious Factor: A Sociologist's Inquiry.*

14

Intelligence and Interpol

Before they left the campus, Hunter took a couple of books from Azriel Moshe's study.

"I think I'll do a bit of reading tonight," he said. "And I don't think Professor Moshe will complain about my borrowing these books."

"What do you have?" asked Weems.

"I've got the *Zohar*, in a translation by someone named Daniel Matt at the Graduate Theological Union in Berkeley. And something called *Major Trends in Jewish Mysticism* by someone named Gershom Sholem. I know the name, somehow. Maybe I read something by him when I was at Berkeley?"

"Sounds like very heavy stuff," replied Weems. "Very deep and ponderous. Not my cup of tea, by any means."

"I want to find out what our intelligence unit and Interpol discovered about the professors on Moshe's team, and about Moshe. Let's get going and see if they've unearthed anything interesting."

They stepped into a police car that was waiting for them and were at their office in twenty minutes.

"Here's our report," said Dan McQuail, a sergeant from the intelligence unit, as he handed Hunter a folder with some papers in it. "We've also been in touch with the FBI and we've integrated what we dug up with whatever we got on these professors here in America and from Interpol to save you some time. You should have the report on your computer."

"Anything interesting?" asked Hunter.

"Nothing that struck my attention," said McQuail, "but I don't know the details of the case. They're each pretty odd. You're dealing with a strange collection of people, no doubt about that."

Hunter and Weems went into Hunter's office.

"Let me get this on my monitor, so we can both look at the finding at the same time," he said to Weems.

Hunter turned on his computer, clicked on a few keys and in a short time the report was on the screen.

Preliminary Findings of an Investigation by the San Francisco Police Intelligence Unit in Collaboration with other American Intelligence Units and Interpol.
Case #: 256338
Tentative case title: The Kabbalah Killing.

Persons Investigated (in alphabetical order):

- Dovet, Jean-Pascal.

- Gerhard, Leon.

- Moshe, Azriel.

- Pagetsky, Svetlana.

- Scelba, Krista.

Dr. Jean-Pascal Dovet, MD

Jean-Pascal Dovet was born in Veules-les-Roses, France in 1954 to Nanette Puce, a hair dresser and Basil Piquer Dovet, an accountant. He studied at Lycee Elihu Dayan in Paris and then obtained the following degrees: BA in zoology and philosophy at the University of Paris, 1972; MD at the University of Paris, 1977; specialization in Neurology at the University of Bologna, 1977 to 1983. He became an assistant professor at the University of Paris after finishing his neurology studies. He married Mathilde Froment, a physician specializing in gastroenterology, in 1984; they divorced in 2002. No children. He is the author of *NeuroKabbalah* published by the Cambridge University Press in 1998 and a number of technical papers on neurological diseases and new technologies. He is not known to the French police or Interpol.

Dr. Leon Gerhard, Ph.D.

Leon Gerhard was born in London in 1950 to Sadie Schmulowitz, a caterer, and Menachim Dov Baer Gerhard, a rabbi. There were seven children in the family. Gerhard obtained the following degrees: BA psychology, 1974, Cambridge University; Ph.D. psychology, Cambridge University, 1977. He also was ordained a rabbi in 1984. He taught psychology at Sussex University from 1977 until 1982; then he moved to the University of California San Francisco, where he taught psychology in the medical school and conducted research. He is the author of *Kabbalah and Psyche,* published by the University of California Press in 1985 and *Mystical Modalities,* published by the University of Minnesota Press, 1990. Leon Gerhard was arrested, and then released, for participating in a protest outside of the Egyptian embassy in San Francisco in 1998. He is not known to Interpol.

Dr. Azriel Moshe, Ph.D.

Azriel Moshe, aka Bernard Moscowitz, is the son of Miriam Iton, an Israeli archaeologist and Albert Moscowitz, an American businessman. He was born in Boston, in 1933. He studied at Central Memorial High School in Boston, graduating in 1950. He received a BA in philosophy from Harvard in 1954 and an MD from Harvard University in 1958. He completed his training in psychiatry at Johns Hopkins University in 1964. He started teaching at the University of California San Francisco Medical School in 1965 as assistant professor. He was promoted to professor in 1975. He changed his name from Bernard Moscowitz to Azriel Moshe in 1980, several years before the publication of his book *The Mind of the Mystic,* published by the Indiana University press. He is known to Interpol. He is thought to have been recruited in the Israeli spy service, the Mossad, around 1980, though it's not known in what capacity he served this agency.

Dr. Svetlana Pagetsky, Ph.D.

Svetlana Akatarina Pagetsky was born in 1970; she was the second child and first daughter of Tatania Noski-Klubnika, a café singer, and Ivan Kisli Pagetsky, a viola player. She was educated at Moscow State University, where she studied political science and history and received her BA there in 1992. She obtained a Ph.D. in history and semiotics at Tartu University in 1996. She was married twice. She married her first husband, Serge Krakmahl-Rubashka, a Russian pediatrician, in 1990. The marriage was annulled in 1991. Her second husband was Dmitri Bulkakov, a Russian businessman, whom she married in 1995. They were divorced a year later. She is the author of *A Thousand Years of Kabbalah: An Historical Overview,* published by Routledge in 2000. She is currently assistant professor of history at Tartu State University. She is not known to Interpol.

Dr. Krista Sophia Scelba, Ph.D.

Krista Sophia Scelba is the daughter of Nadia Ruggine-Schlang, a school teacher, and Ruggiero Scelba, an orthopedic surgeon. She was born in 1953 in Milan and was educated at Liceo Agostino de Lombardo-Ladro, from which she graduated in 1970. She received her BA in law at the University of Milan in 1975 and a Ph.D. in sociology from the University of Rome in 1979. She is the author of a book whose title in its English translation is *The Kabbalah Brotherhood: A Sociological Inquiry.* The book was originally published in Italian by Rizzoli and in its English translation by

Oxford University Press. She was married for five years to a professor at the University of Milan, Nello Tacchino, who, according to official records, committed suicide. She is not known to Interpol.

Coroner's Report (Summary)

Victim killed from knife wound to back that glanced off ribcage and nicked the heart. Death approximately at noon. Victim was seated when knifed since knife wound was vertical in nature. Also, reason to suggest killer was left-handed since wound was on left-hand side of back.

"Well, well. Isn't that interesting," said Hunter. "Azriel Moshe was originally Bernard Moskowitz and Professor Scelba was married to a husband who committed suicide. She certainly didn't volunteer that information. That's something we have to think about."

"You think she might have killed her husband?" asked Weems. "And then, since she got away with it once, decided to kill Moshe for having dumped her. It would be a matter of if at first you *do* succeed, try, try again."

"It's the 'try again' part that we have to worry about in this case," replied Hunter. "I'm glad we're having all of the professors protected. It pays to play it safe. The only reason the killer might strike again would be to prevent someone who might have seen something from talking. The professors we interrogated might be in danger because they didn't realize they saw something, or knew something that they didn't realize was important or they were trying to fool us."

"It wouldn't be the first time a witness who knew something that he thought was trivial didn't tell us and made a fatal mistake," said Weems.

"You're sure they're all being well guarded, Talcott?" added Hunter.

"We've got men surrounding their houses. We're not taking any chances," said Weems.

"Good," replied Hunter. "I'm going home now and read the *Zohar* and find out what I can about the Kabbalah."

"From what those professors told us this afternoon, I don't imagine you'll be able to make much sense of it—gobbledygook on Ein Sof and the Sefirot and the unerasable names and all kinds of other mumbo-jumbo," said Weems.

"We'll see what I learn this evening and then what happens tomorrow," said Hunter. "I'm looking forward to what I imagine will be a fascinating evening. And I expect, given the nature of the people we're dealing with, a most interesting morning tomorrow. Anything can happen."

"Yes," said Weems. "That's what I'm afraid of."

Cabalism was a movement of profound mystical faith fused to and steeped in the superstitions and occult preoccupations of pre-Middle Ages. It was a minor but meaningful system of thought and experience, a pious attempt to fathom the awesome, fearful mysteries of God and creation. Originally, cabalism meant the Oral Tradition; in the twelfth century, Jewish mystics adopted the term, claiming an unbroken link between their ideas and those of ancient days.

Cabalists claimed that their revelation was part and parcel of Scripture. But cabalism's divinations and abracadabra, its intricate numerology (see Gematria), remained in the shadowland until the eighth century A.D., when *The Book of Formation* appeared in Italy.

Not until *The Book of Splendour* (the *Zohar*) appeared in Spain in the thirteenth century did a formidable metaphysical text on cabalism appear. Two hundred years later the great Renaissance humanist Pico della Mirandola translated the *Zohar* into Latin. And not until the seventeenth century did cabalism become a movement of consequence.

The cabalists held that reason alone could never penetrate the exalted mystical experience involved in their perception of God and His mysteries. Esoteric formulas, numerological acrobatics, theological mumbo jumbo went into the cabalists' efforts to apprehend God's will. And many a cabalistic omen or prophecy excitedly hailed the imminent appearance of the Messiah and the Day of Judgement. (1968: 60-61)

- Leo Rosten, *The Joys of Yiddish*

15

Confession Time

LEON GERHARD TELLS HUNTER SOMETHING QUITE SHOCKING

Everyone had gathered together at around 9:45 AM in the seminar room. Solomon Hunter, Talcott Weems, and four policemen, who stood behind each of the professors were all crowded into the seminar room together. Hunter sat at one end of the table. To his immediate left, was Jean-Pascal Dovet, next to Dovet was Krista Scelba, and next to her was Talcott Weems, who was at the other end of the table. To Hunter's immediate right sat Svetlana Pagetsky, and next to her, Leon Gerhard.

"We're outnumbered," said Jean-Pascal Dovet, smiling. "But why such a show of force?" he asked Hunter.

"There's safety in numbers," replied Hunter.

"For you or for us?" Dovet asked nervously. He was wearing a gray turtleneck shirt, a pair of black trousers, and some Teva river sandals.

"Why are we here?" asked Krista. "Are you going to put us that room again and interrogate each of us for a second time?" She was wearing semi-translucent white makeup, had purple eye liner above her eyes, and false eyelashes. Her lipstick was also purple, and she wore a dark green dress and a heavy necklace of large silver beads. She wore snakeskin shoes with four inch heels.

"I hope not, Krista," said Svetlana. "It was so painful talking about Azriel's death yesterday. I don't know if I can bear to do so again." She was wearing a long tan dress and Birkenstock sandals. Her hair was pulled back and coiled on top of her head.

"I don't think that will be necessary," said Hunter.

"Not necessary?" asked Leon Gerhard. "Does that mean you've discovered something? Have you, by chance, figured out who killed Azriel?"

"Let's say I'm making progress on the case," Hunter replied. "It's a very complicated one, like most murders. But we've learned a few things from talking with you and from our intelligence unit and the Interpol."

"Do you think I might have a word with you in private?" asked Krista Scelba. "I hate to interrupt you, but it's important."

Her face showed signs of stress.

"Let's go to the room where you waited for us," said Hunter. "We'll be back in a few minutes," he said to the others in the room. "Weems, please join us."

Weems got up and joined Hunter and Krista Scelba as they walked over to the room where the members of the team had waited the day before. When they sat down, Scelba burst into tears.

"It's all over," she said. "I confess to killing Azriel Moshe. In a moment of madness, I plunged the knife into his back. I. . . I was just overwhelmed by my hatred of him. He had cast me off without a second thought, without as much as an apology. He was. . . he was a monster."

She then burst out crying, her body throbbing. The tears flowed down her face, messing up her makeup and making her face look horrid.

Hunter watched her impassively.

"I have to say that I'm a bit surprised by your confession," he replied. "But I don't know whether, at this moment in time, I can accept it."

"You don't believe me?" she asked, incredulously.

"It isn't a matter of accepting it or not. There's a process of discussion and analysis that I need to go through with your colleagues, and until that is completed, I'm afraid I can't accept your confession.

"I. . . I don't know what to say," she replied.

"Let's go back and we'll see what happens as we discuss the events that took place yesterday at noon," said Hunter softly.

"Yes, I understand," she said weakly.

"Tell me," Hunter asked, "Was Azriel Moshe sitting or standing when you stabbed him?"

"Sitting," she replied.

"And did you stab him on the left hand part of his back or the right hand part?" he asked.

She paused for a moment.

"On the left hand part, I believe. I can't be sure since I was in a great hurry. After I stabbed him, I raced out of the room, went back to my office, and continued my chat with Jean-Pascal. I had left him waiting on the line. The whole thing took less than two minutes. He must not have died immediately but, I imagine, crawled to the center of his office and collapsed on the floor, where he tried to leave a sign of some sort with his blood."

"I see," said Hunter.

Just then there was a knock on the door, and Officer Abe Kook opened it.

"Sorry to interrupt you, but another member of the team asked to speak with you privately."

"Hmm," said Hunter. "This is most unusual. Okay, please bring Professor Scelba back to the room where her colleagues are waiting."

As she left, Leon Gerhard entered the room. He grasped her arm to indicate his support for her. She looked at him and smiled weakly.

"Won't you sit down," said Hunter.

"Listen, I've got to get this off my chest," said Gerhard, who stood impatiently. He looked tense and his eyes were shifting around rapidly. "I killed Azriel Gerhard. I thought I could work with him, even though he had stolen my ideas and used them as the basis for his book on Kabbalah. But I was wrong, and with each meeting my hatred for him grew more and more intense. Finally I couldn't stand it any more. So when we finished our meeting and broke for lunch, I slipped into his office and when he wasn't looking, I stuck that knife in his back."

"Was he standing or sitting when you killed him?" asked Hunter.

"What? What do you mean?" he asked. He seemed surprised by the question and confused.

"I just want to get the details straight," replied Hunter.

"He was standing," said Gerhard. "He was looking for some book in his bookcase when I caught him by surprise. He uttered a short gurgle and immediately fell to the ground. I left right away. I take it that he didn't die immediately but tried to pull the knife out of his back but couldn't and, with a bloody hand, tried to write something on the rug."

"You saw the mark he made? Was it part of a Hebrew letter?"

"There was too little to say," replied Gerhard. "It could have been the beginning of a B or a V or a K."

"I see," said Hunter. "Why did you wait so long to confess? Why didn't you do so immediately?"

"I was crazed," Gerhard replied. "My passion had overwhelmed my good sense and I was, for a short while, unrepentant. I had a visitor last night, who looked to me as a rabbi. It was a wake-up call. I'm a rabbi—how can I possibly assume the mantle of a teacher and a holy man when I've acted so basely? When my visitor was looking to me for answers, I realized that I couldn't give her any when I had this crime plaguing my conscience. I have done something terrible and this confession is a first step towards paying for my sinful behavior. I hope Azriel, poor man, will forgive me, if he is in heaven and looking down on us."

"I understand," said Hunter.

"You can arrest me now," said Gerhard. "I'll sign whatever document you ask me to. I'm the guilty one."

He had a pleased look on his face as he made his confession—the look of a person who is suddenly released from a terrible burden.

"If you don't mind, I'd like to wait before I do anything. There is a process that we need to go through before I accept anyone's confession of guilt."

"Yes... yes, I understand," said Gerhard. "You have your own rituals, or maybe the term 'bureaucratic routine' is more accurate for this kind of thing. I can wait. Especially since I have no choice in the matter. But you need not trouble yourself or any of my colleagues, since I have admitted that I killed Azriel Moshe."

At that moment there was a loud knock on the door and Office Abe Kook opened the door.

"Sorry to interrupt you like this," he said, "but the Russian professor—we think she just tried to kill herself. Or was going to kill someone else."

"What?" exclaimed Hunter. "What happened?"

"The secretary had arranged for some coffee and donuts to be served," said Kook. "After Professor Pagetsky got a cup of coffee and a donut, she suddenly exclaimed 'I must do it now' and reached into her handbag. She pulled out a small revolver. Officer Kipper, who was standing behind her, saw what she was doing, grabbed her and we took the gun away from her. She then burst out crying, hysterically, and I ran over here to see what you want us to do with her."

Hunter turned to Leon Gerhard.

"I'm afraid we're going to have to end this interview prematurely. I'll have Officer Kook escort you back to the seminar room. I'd like to talk with Professor Pagetsky immediately."

"I understand," said Gerhard, as he left the room. "Everything is falling apart... I can see that now."

A couple of minutes later, Svetlana Pagetsky appeared. She was crying hysterically as she entered the room. She sat down and continued to cry for several more minutes. With a deep breath, she stopped crying and regained her composure.

"What a fool I've been," she said, weakly. "I must apologize for my behavior, but I've lost my grip on rationality in the last two days. I hardly slept last night and had a strange dream."

"Just calm down and relax," said Hunter, softly. "These things happen when there's a murder. People involved in the case often become terribly upset and do crazy things."

"Yes, yes... that's true," she replied. "But, you see, there was a reason for my behavior—a sense of overpowering guilt that I felt, a sense that any hope I had for a decent life was now gone."

"Why was that?" asked Hunter.

"Because, you see," she said, pausing and taking a deep breath, "it was I who killed Azriel Moshe! I was insane with hatred and jealousy, and so I stabbed him."

"Where did you stab him?" asked Hunter.

"In the back," she replied. "There was a knife sticking out of his back. We all saw that when we heard his secretary screaming and rushed into his office."

"But where precisely? On the left hand side of his back or the right hand side? Or in the middle?"

"I... I can't remember," she said, nervously.

"Did you feel the knife hit one of his ribs or did it go straight in?" asked Hunter.

"I was so overwrought and nervous that I can't remember. I was in a great hurry, since I didn't want anyone to find me in the room with him, so I stuck the knife in and immediately left. My mind has gone blank, actually. I remember nothing, except that I stabbed him. It was as if I were in a trance. And this morning, when we gathered together in the seminar room, I suddenly felt so remorseful that I decided to kill myself. But one of your officers grabbed me and prevented me from doing so."

"How do we know you didn't intend to use the gun to kill someone else? Maybe you had that in mind?" asked Hunter.

"No! Believe me! It was only Azriel who I hated, who drove me to this act of madness. And now — now my life is ruined," she said, as she burst out crying again.

"I think it would be best if you returned to the seminar room and quieted down a bit. Maybe a cup of coffee and a donut will help," said Hunter.

"Aren't you going to arrest me now?" she asked, incredulously. "Isn't that what happens when someone confesses to a murder?"

"The arrest will come in due time," said Hunter.

"Weems," he said, turning to his colleague, "will you kindly escort Professor Pagetsky back to the seminar room. And while you're there, why not bring Professor Dovet here. Let's see what he has to say about the events that have taken place."

"Will do," said Weems.

He walked over to the professor, who was sitting with a glum look on her face.

"Please come with me," he said. "You need to calm down and relax a bit."

"Yes, you're right," she said. She got up and left the room with Talcott Weems.

Several minutes later, Weems appeared with Jean-Pascal Dovet.

"It's a surprise that you asked to see me, since I was going to ask to speak with you, privately, before you met with us," he said. "But the past two days have been full of surprises. Most unpleasant ones, alas."

"Yes," said Hunter.

"I have something to tell you that will, I imagine, surprise you," Dovet added.

"You're going to tell me that you killed Azriel Moshe," said Hunter. "Is that correct?"

Dovet had a look on amazement on his face.

"But how did you know? What did I do to give myself away?" Dovet asked. "I thought I had worked it out perfectly. Where did I go wrong?"

"May I ask you to reconstruct the killing," replied Hunter. "In some detail."

"Reconstruct?" said Dovet. "What do you mean reconstruct?"

"Was Moshe standing or sitting when you stabbed him?" asked Hunter.

"Why standing, of course!" replied Dovet. "I asked him to find a book for me and he got up from his desk and was about to look for the book when I plunged the knife into his back. Then I left immediately."

"I see," said Hunter. "Do you remember whether the knife hit a rib or went in cleanly?"

Dovet paused for a moment, taken aback.

"It hit a rib," he said slowly, "and then plunged in further."

"I see," said Hunter. "And why did you kill Moshe? And why yesterday?"

"I became angrier and angrier with him," replied Dovet. "I despised his mocking tone, his attitude of superiority, the nasty jokes he made about me, and the way he treated the other members of the team. Finally, I reached the boiling point and exploded. It was an irrational action, I recognize that. But there are times when we become, for one reason or another, so angry and upset that we act irrationally."

"I see," said Hunter.

"Of course, once I killed him I immediately felt enormous remorse and an overwhelming sense of despair. Not only had I killed Azriel, I had, so to speak, killed my future. At first I thought I would get away with it. Nobody had seen me enter his office or leave it. The whole thing only took two minutes at the most. I did it while I was supposedly holding the phone during my conversation with Krista. But then, last night, I was thinking about what I had done. Every murder is a multiple killing. You kill a person but you also kill your future and also the hopes and love of that person's friends and family, so each killing is a multiple murder."

Dovet breathed heavily. His face had a pained look on it.

"At least my confession with spare my colleagues further agony," he added. "That, I believe, is one good thing I have done for them. You can arrest me now. I'll sign a confession and that will put matters to rest."

"I should inform you," Hunter said, "that each of your colleagues has confessed to murdering Azriel Moshe!"

"What? That's impossible!" he cried. "Each of us?"

Then he stopped and thought for a moment. The tension on his face gave way to something approaching a smile.

"So, Inspector. The tragedy looks like it will end in a comedy."

"Let's go back to the seminar room and I'll see what sense I can make of everything," said Hunter. "I don't know whether the right word is comedy or farce."

The fulfilment of man's task in this world is connected by Luria, as well as by all the other Safed Kabbalists, with the doctrine of metempsychosis, or transmigration of the soul. In the later development of the school of Safed, this remarkable doctrine has been elaborated in great detail, and Hayim Vital's *Sefer Ha-Gilgulim*, or "Book of Transmigrations," in which he gave a systematic description of Luria's doctrine of metempsychosis, is the final product of a long and important development in Kabbalistic thought. (1946:280-281)

- Gershom Scholem, *Major Trends in Jewish Mysticism*

16

The False Messiah

Hunter returned to the seminar room with Jean-Pascal Dovet.

"This has been quite a morning," Hunter said. "Quite a morning."

"I've been a cop for thirty years," added Weems, "and I've never seen anything like it!"

"What do you mean?" asked Svetlana Pagetsky. "You've solved the crime, so to speak, and your work is done. You can arrest the murderer, go to your office, write your report about poor Azriel's murder, and that will be that."

"It's not quite so easy," replied Hunter. "During the last hour, one way or another, each of you has somehow managed to speak with me privately. And each of you has had something very interesting to tell me."

"Which was?" asked Dovet.

"Each of you confessed to murdering Azriel Moshe!"

"What?" said Krista Scelba. "The others, too?"

"Dovet confessed? Preposterous!" exclaimed Leon Gerhard. "I can't believe that Jean-Pascal would kill anyone."

"Nor can I believe that Svetlana killed Azriel. It doesn't make sense," said Jean-Pascal.

"The others confessed, but I'm telling the truth," said Svetlana Pagetsky. "You needn't take Krista's confession, or any of the confessions—other than mine, that is—seriously."

"Stop trying to protect me, Svetlana!" cried Krista Scelba. "I know that Inspector Hunter thinks Leon did it, but I'm telling the truth. He didn't do it and I did do it! The rest of you are lying, to protect someone else!"

"I've had four confessions," said Hunter. "Four of you confessed and three of you, I'm certain, were lying. The question is—which one of you was telling the truth?"

"Let me tell you my thoughts about the case—so far. What can we be certain of? Only that Azriel Moshe was stabbed in the back and, as the coroner's report certifies, died from the stabbing—from the loss of blood and from a nick on the heart. After each of you confessed, I asked you some questions, such as whether Azriel was sitting or standing when you stabbed him, and whether your blade hit one of his ribs or went in clean. Three of you answered incorrectly, whether because your were unable or unwilling. You hemmed and hawed and did anything you could to stall for time so you could figure how to answer to my question and not give yourself away."

"I've thought about the tangled set of relationships that exists among you. Jean-Pascal seems to be crazy about Svetlana Pagetsky and shows it, in a perverse way, by acting hostile. In Azriel Moshe's journal, however, I found a comment that Jean-Pascal is 'crazy' about her. Svetlana Pagetsky, on the other hand, is in love with Krista Scelba, which Jean-Pascal didn't realize because Krista didn't realize it either. Despite all her bluff, Svetlana is actually timid. The reason her two marriages didn't take was because she didn't realize, at the time, that she was a lesbian. When I asked her about Krista Scelba, there was, for a brief instant on

Svetalana's face the look of a woman in love. It quickly passed, but I took notice of it."

"Poor thing," said Krista Scelba, softly.

"Yes, poor thing. But Professor Scelba also was the victim of unrequited love. First, I was told that she was having a relationship with Azriel Moshe, who dumped her, as we would say here in America, for Svetlana. In this respect, he was the victim of unrequited love, or, perhaps, unsatisfied passions. But you, Professor Scelba, also had your own tragedy—namely that you were crazy about Leon Gerhard, who happens to be gay, though he is discreet about it."

"I find your analysis...." said Gerhard. "Oh, never mind. This story about everyone's unrequited love is getting boring."

"But you, too, were in love, but with someone who didn't know it and wouldn't have been interested, if he did know it!"

"Azriel?" asked Svetlana.

"No, Jean-Pascal!" replied Hunter.

"Me?" said Jean-Pascal, incredulously. "I had no idea! This analysis is absolutely crazy. You've lost your mind."

"You were so involved with your dreams about Svetlana that you didn't notice that Leon Gerhard was attracted to you," said Hunter. "So, the first thing I had to deal with was the fact that everyone on this team was in love with someone who either didn't know it, or if they did know it, wasn't interested. And there was the matter of which of the women had been, were, or weren't involved with Azriel Moshe and what consequences those relationships might have had."

"The problem I faced involved which one of you might be the killer. Moshe had, so it seems, dumped Krista Scelba. And had prevented her from getting a chair at Yale."

As he said this, Hunter looked at her and noticed the muscles of her face tighten.

"Then, he had stolen ideas from Leon Gerhard—ideas which Gerhard suggested were behind Moshe's book on Kabbalah that made his name. He had, Svetlana suggested, been 'forceful' one night, in Tartu, when they had sex. And he was pressing her for sexual favors—not recognizing that she was a lesbian. And what about Dovet? Nothing, except that he was insanely jealous of Azriel Moshe and upset about his relations with Svetlana Paget-sky. Everyone had a motive."

Hunter paused, and picked up a book from the seminar table.

"Last night, I read a couple of books, which I took from Azriel Moshe's study. One was the *Zohar* and another was a book on the essentials of the Kabbalah. In the *Zohar* one passage caught my attention. It's about murder. Let me read it to you."

He picked up Moshe's copy of the *Zohar* and opened it.

"This is what I read," said Hunter. "I'll skip a few passages here and there."

Out of the dregs of wine,
. . . a fungus emerged, a cluster
male and female together,
red as a rose,
expanding in many directions and paths.
The male is called Sama'el
his female always included within him. . .
The female of Sama'el is called Serpent
Woman of Whoredom. . .
She bedecks herself with all kinds of jewelry
like an abhorrent prostitute posing on the corner to seduce
men. . .
her face white and red
six trinkets dangling from her ears
her bed covered with fabric from Egypt
on her neck all the jewels of the East. . .
This fool follows her, drinks from the cup of wine,
fornicated with her, deviates after her.
What does she do?
She leaves him sleeping in bed.
She ascends, denounces him, obtains permission, and descends.

That fool wakes up and plans to play with her as before.
But she removes her decorations
and turns into a powerful warrior confronting him.
Arrayed in armor of flashing fire,
his awesome terror vibrates the victim's body and soul.
He is full of fearsome eyes;
in his hand a sharp-edged sword drips bitter drops.
He kills that fool and flings him into hell.

Everyone had become mute. As he finished, Jean-Pascal Dovet, Krista Scelba and Leon Gerhard looked at Svetlana with astonished looks on their faces.

"Lilith!" said Krista Scelba. "That verse. It describes Lilith."

"But it doesn't describe me," cried Svetlana. "I've confessed to killing Azriel, but I'm not the Lilith figure you describe. It doesn't describe me!"

"No! It doesn't!" Hunter said. "You may pose as a beauty queen, but you like the natural look. You're not the Lilith figure in this group."

"But that leaves...." said Jean-Pascal.

"Yes, me!" said Krista Scelba. "When I confessed to killing Azriel, I was telling the truth, unlike the rest of you, who were trying to protect someone else. Poor Svetlana... trying to protect me. That was most kind. The things we do when we're in love and when we are ruled by blind hatred. Incredible. I had been humiliated by Azriel and my career had been damaged because of his lies. I despised him. No, worse than that, I hated him and two nights ago I had a dream about Azriel. In this dream, he wore a long white robe with gold threads in it. He claimed to be the Messiah. I knew then that my duty was to kill him. We've had too many false Messiahs, too many. In that dream, the 78 names of God were revealed to me. I was given a task by El Shaddei— to rid the world of Azriel Moshe, that False Messiah. 'No more false messiahs,' God said to me, speaking through a cloud. And I have! You can do what you want with me because my body is now irrelevant. My soul is now abandoning my body and moving to a higher astral level."

With that she slumped over in a dead faint.

Shortly after the police took her away for psychiatric observation. The other suspects, badly shaken, began to depart. Leon Gerhard came over to Solomon Hunter.

"Inspector Hunter," he said. "I must congratulate you for a remarkable display of analysis. It was worthy of a Talmudic scholar. You should know that there is a long tradition in Judaism which holds that studying Kabbalah is dangerous. That's why some rabbis argued that nobody should attempt studying Kabbalah until they are forty. Other rabbis, of course, disagreed with them and said Kabbalah could be studied at twenty. Whatever the case, the notion that delving into the mysteries of Kabbalah is perilous has been with us for a long time. Kabbalists argue that we lost the hidden knowledge that Adam and Eve had when they ate from the tree of knowledge and were cast out of Eden. Kabbalah, it was believed, would bring us back. But the return to Paradise was full of peril.

"In the Talmud, there is a story that illustrates the danger of learning the secrets that enable us to return to paradise. In this story, four rabbis entered paradise: Rabbi Ben Azzai, Rabbi Ben Zoma, Rabbi Elisha ben Avuyah, and Rabbi Akiva. Rabbi Ben Azzai glimpsed paradise and died. Rabbi Ben Zoma glimpsed it and went mad. Rabbi ben Avuyah, also known as Aher, cut the plants he saw—a metaphoric way of saying that he became a heretic. And only Rabbi Akiva emerged unscathed from the experience.

"This terrible murder, in which we've all been involved," he continued, "makes me think of that story, for everyone on the team was searching, as Kabbalists would have it, even if they didn't know it, for secrets that would reveal paradise to them. Azriel Moshe died; Krista Scelba went mad. What will happen to Svetlana and Jean-Pascal and myself remains to be seen. Whether any of us—or all of us—will leave our faith is hard to say. And what, may I ask, will you call this case?"

"I don't know," said Hunter. "Maybe the Kabbalah Case or the Kabbalah Murder?"

"If you don't think it's too forward of me, may I suggest a title?" said Gerhard.

Hunter smiled.

"Why not?" he replied.

"I'd call it 'The Kabbalah Killings," he said.

"How come the plural? Why killings?" asked Hunter.

"Because," said Gerhard, "The death of Azriel Moshe is only part of the story. One person has been murdered, that's true. But I fear, maybe some of us in the team may have lost our faith in Kabbalah, in religion, and in human goodness. I'm afraid that our faith in these things has been killed."

"The Kabbalah Killings it is," said Hunter. "But before you become despondent and lose your faith in human kindness, remember that each of your colleagues was willing to take the murder rap because of someone he or she loved. So the power of love is the most important thing you should remember from this sad story. It's as much a part of the story as poor Krista Scelba's madness. And remember, also, this Rabbi Akiva of yours. He glimpsed paradise and emerged in peace. In time, when you get over this terrible event, you'll find that you have done the same thing."

Bibliography

Boyarin, Daniel. 1994 *Intertextuality and the Reading of Midrash.* Bloomingon, IN: Indiana University Press.

Eliade, Mircea. 1961 *The Sacred and The Profane: The Nature of Religion.* New York: Harper & Row.

Lenski, Gerhard. 1963 *The Religious Factor: A Sociologist's Inquiry* Garden City, NY: Anchor.

Matt, Daniel C. 1983 (Transl. Daniel C. Matt) *Zohar: The Book of Enlightenment.* Mahwah, NJ: Paulist Press

Matt, Daniel C. 1996 *The Essential Kabbalah: The Heart of Jewish Mysticism.* San Francisco: Harper/San Francisco

Rosten, Leo. 1971. *The Joys of Yiddish.* Harmondsworth, UK: Penguin

Scholem, Gershom. 1946. *Major Trends in Jewish Mysticism.* New York: Schocken

About the Author

Arthur Asa Berger is professor emeritus of Broadcast and Electronic Communication Arts at San Francisco State University, where he taught from 1965 until 2003. An improper Bostonian, he grew up in Roxbury, Massachusetts (a part of Boston) and went to Roxbury Memorial High School for Boys from 1947-1950. Then he attended the University of Massachusetts in Amherst, where he was awarded a BA in literature and philosophy in 1954. He received an MA degree in journalism and creative writing from the University of Iowa in 1956. He was drafted shortly after graduating from Iowa and served in the US Army in the Military District of Washington in Washington DC, where he was a feature writer and speech writer in the District's Public Information Office. He also wrote high school sports for *The Washington Post* on weekend evenings.

Berger spent a year touring Europe after he got out of the Army and then studied at the University of Minnesota, where he received a Ph.D. in American Studies in 1965. He wrote his dissertation on Al Capp's comic strip *Li'l Abner.* In 1963-64, he had a Fulbright to Italy and taught at the University of Milan. He spent a year as visiting professor at the Annenberg School for Communication at The University of Southern California, in Los Angeles in 1984.

He is the author of numerous articles, book reviews, and books on the mass media, popular culture, humor, and everyday life. Among his books are *The Genius of the Jewish Joke, Media & Society, Making Sense of Media, The Art of Comedy Writing,* and

Video Games: A Popular Culture Phenomenon. He has also written a number of academic mysteries: *The Hamlet Case, Postmortem for a Postmodernist, The Mass Comm Murders: Five Media Theorists Self-Destruct,* and *Durkheim is Dead: Sherlock Holmes is Introduced to Sociological Theory.* His books have been translated into seven languages and he has lectured in more than a dozen countries in the course of his career.

Berger is married, has two children and two grandchildren, and lives in Mill Valley, California. He enjoys travel and dining in ethnic restaurants. He can be reached by e-mail at: aberger@sfsu.edu or arthurasaberger@yahoo.com.

PulpLit Publishing

PulpLit Publishing's mission is to publish innovative fiction and literature. As well as books, PulpLit Publishing publishes a small online magazine devoted to literary criticism and thoughtful analysis of pop culture. Particularly interested in genre fiction that transcends genre, literary analysis that goes beyond mundane formalism, and art and poetry which excite and stimulate the mind, PulpLit Publishing publishes a PulpLit online every quarter.

For more information, including the current issue of PulpLit, please visit us online at **PulpLit.com**.